BOUNDED

BOOK III

NICOLETTE JOHNSON

DAY n Night
Publishing LLC

Love isn't for everyone,

but when you find it;

Hold tight…

Because it will be a hell of a ride

PRELUDE

TYRA

Eight Months Earlier

"Why are you looking at me like that?"

"Take that stupid scowl off your face! Now!"

The devil has entered her soul. I must get him out NOW!

But, how?

But, why her?

"Leave my baby alone."

"Please leave her alone."

"Leave me alone. Please, leave us alone," I beg silently as I pray on my knees, rocking back and forth. "God, you must hear my prayers."

"Water…" the voice keeps whispering to me. *"Water…"*

She keeps crying and screaming, and she just won't stop. The voice keeps whispering to me, and it won't stop. Just make it stop.

"STOP IT!" I screamed at Annabelle. But she keeps screaming. "Please, stop crying."

"Please make it stop. Make the screaming stop. I can't take the screaming anymore," I beg on the top of my lungs.

"Please."

"*Water... Tyra. Water...*" the voice keeps insisting.

"I don't know what you mean. Please tell me what you want," I announce to the voice, begging for any type of response.

"*Water...put me in Water...*" the voice demands.

I walk into the bathroom and sit on the floor. I put my knees to my chest and place my head in between my knees, rocking myself back and forth. It won't stop. I don't know what to do anymore. Please just make it stop. I beg silently to myself.

"*Turn on the water, Tyra.*"

"Okay," I snap back while Annabelle still screaming at the top of her lungs. I get up off the floor and fill the tub with water.

"*Come get me...*" the voice demands.

"No, she won't stop crying. I can't take the crying anymore. Don't make me go in there."

"*She will...in the water,*" the voice promises.

She will? I question more to myself than to the voice. Why didn't I think of this before? Giving her a soothing hot bath will make a world of difference. I can finally have peace and quiet.

I walk out of the bathroom with purpose, my head pounding from all the screaming. I enter Annabelle's room. Her room has purple dragonflies painted on the wall with fireflies buzzing around them. There are stars scattered all around the ceiling, and for a moment, I think this is the happiest place on earth, but then Annabelle's screaming brings me back to reality.

My very own hell.

I bend over her crib and pull her into my arms. Bradley will never understand the torture I suffer every day he is gone. Annabelle only cries with me. She never shed a tear with him.

She won't stop. Even now, trying to soothe her is like committing an exorcism on her. Like the demon himself refuses to let me comfort her.

Well, fuck him and fuck her!!!

I walk into the bathroom, determined to shut her the fuck up. I take her clothes off and pamper, dropping everything on the floor.

"*Close and lock the door,*" the voice requests.

"Okay." I turn and shut the door and lock it. I then place Annabelle in the water. She continues to scream.

"Fuck, shut the hell up. Fucking devil, get the fuck out of her!"

I push her under the water, and for a moment, everything is silent, peace overwhelming me, and I no longer hear the screaming, the piercing sounds of wailing until...

Bang. Bang. Bang.

"Open the door, Tyra. Open the fucking door!" Bradley demands.

Bang. Bang. Bang.

"No, the devil is leaving her once and for all. This is the only way. You see...she stopped crying. Thank God, she finally stopped..."

The door crashes open, slamming into the wall. I feel hands ripping me from the floor. My body slams against the wall, and everything turns black.

Finally, the piercing sounds of wailing are gone...

3

CHAPTER 1

AMELIA

PRESENT DAY

*I*t's almost summer, but you couldn't tell by the gloomy, foggy atmosphere. It's early in the morning, and everything is calm and weary. The grass is dewy, and the streets are peaceful. It's my favorite time of day to run in the downtown area of historic Savannah. The stores are closed, and the nightlife has ended. All the sins of yesterday will fester until tonight. For now, I take my time running and enjoying the peacefulness of the city.

I'm listening to 'I Don't Wanna Live Forever' by ZAYN and Taylor Swift. This song directly contradicts how I should be feeling, but I don't care. I find music to be my escape. There's music for all emotions, and I rely heavily on this release each waking morning.

Dance is another escape for me, and I cherish every move like it's my last breath to breathe. People say we all go through something in our lives, and how we react to it will dictate our future. In the past, I would have found that a shocking revelation. But, after I lost both my parents when I was only sixteen and almost my sister two years ago, I find myself cherishing the little things, like watching the birds find their next meal or enjoying the scenery of such beautiful landscape in the historic squares.

I pick up my pace to get my heart rate up. I find the more I run, the lower my anxiety is. I lost track of how many therapists I've seen or how many different activities they've told me to try. After a while, I gave up on the professionals and started thinking for myself.

My wonderful sister, Lily, has been by my side since day one. Even when she married Jason, she still looked out for me. He even looks out for me like a brother protecting his sister. His own sister, Dianella, is my best friend. She's been a godsend, and I honestly don't know how I would have made it through school each day without her.

Dianella and I work at The Grind, a joint owner with her brother. We both manage the small quaint coffee shop. Besides running and dancing, it's the highlight of my day. Working helps me take my mind off everything, and running and dancing help me center myself, a win-win situation.

I continue to run through the downtown area and make it to Forsyth Park, the heart and soul of the city. I love Forsyth Park because it's so relaxing. When I'm not running or working or taking classes at Georgia University, then I'm lying in the park with my eyes closed, imagining possibilities.

I decide to run the entire perimeter of the park and head back towards my loft. When I make it halfway around, I trip over something on the ground. I feel myself about to collide with the sidewalk, but no, not the sidewalk. Something catches me from hitting the hard concrete. Strong arms embrace me, and a hard chest comforts me. I look up into the eyes of my savior, and it's no other than Bradley Philips. He has beautiful, eerily serene grey eyes. His face is rugged with dark facial hair, and his features are alluring. He has the skin color of warm caramel mixed with milk chocolate, and I just sit there in his large biceps because I don't know what else to do.

He lifts me up and steadies me on my feet. I take a deep breath and smell his masculine musk mixed with fresh soap and sandalwood.

Oh, how I remember that smell from the first time I met him at Kim's and Ryan's vacation home. He stood at six foot four, tall and solid. He keeps a low brush cut with never-ending waves. He was absolutely gorgeous then, and now he is stunning to every woman he crosses, including me. He is well-mannered and very ambitious. When I saw him last, he had the cuties little bundle of joy I've ever seen, Annabelle.

She has his eyes and beautiful curly hair with cheeks made of little clouds. When I held her in my arms, she gave me a smile that made me fall in love with her instantly.

"Hey, Amelia. Are you okay?" he asks me with a deep seductive voice. I don't say anything right away because I'm hypnotized by his handsome features. "Amelia, did you hurt yourself?" he asks again, but slightly firm.

"Uh, no. I'm fine," brushing myself off with my hands. "I'm sorry, I wasn't paying attention to where I was going."

"No, it's okay. I happened to look up at the last minute and saw you heading straight for the baby stroller. I didn't want you to hurt yourself."

"Ah, yes, of course. Thank you." I look down at the stroller and realize Annabelle is staring at me. Probably because of the bright colors I'm wearing. "Hi, Annabelle. How's the sweetest girl on the planet?" I gush as I lean down to absorb her brightly beautiful soul.

"She's growing so fast. I'm having trouble keeping up," Bradley gushes over his precious daughter.

"She's about eight months now, right?" I ask as he looks surprised at my observation of remembering his daughter's age. I bend down a little more to play with her tiny little hands.

"Uh, yes. Annabelle will be nine months in a couple of weeks. Then, before I know it, she will be off to college and exploring the world."

"Yes, time flies. You have to cherish the little things because it doesn't last forever."

"You got that right. So, you're out for a morning run?" Bradley asks with enthusiasm in his tone.

"Yeah, it helps with clearing my head before I tackle the day. What about you?"

"I bring Annabelle to the park every day to get fresh air before I head into work. Also, it gives me time to bond with her since I work long hours, and she's asleep when I get home."

"Oh, I certainly get it. It will also give her mom time to take a break. My sister has triplets, as you know, so I understand all too well when a mother needs time for herself." He physically tenses up at the statement I just made, but it disappears just as quickly, like it never happened. But I noticed the change.

Changing the conversation, "So, are you headed home, or are you still running?"

I decided not to push, but there is definitely a story there. "Yes, I'm headed home. I need to help Dianella with the morning rush at The Grind and then get ready for class later today."

"You're in school?"

"Yes, I attend Georgia University. I'm getting my degree in Nursing and a minor in Performing Arts."

"Wow, impressive. So, you like helping people?"

"Yeah, basically a part of my nature."

"I can tell." I feel myself blushing at the compliment. "I attend Georgia University as well. I'm getting my degree in Business Administration, specializing in Accounting. Maybe I'll see you around."

"Yeah, maybe," having nothing else to say, I prepare to turn around and continue on my run.

"Uh, Amelia?"

"Yes?" turning back around.

"Can I call you sometime?" I thought he would never ask since he never asked for my number four months ago.

"Of course. You have your phone?"

"Yes, here." He hands me his phone, and I put my contact information in it. I then hand the phone back to him. "Thanks."

"Anytime," playing it off like it isn't the biggest deal in the world that he actually wants to talk to me. So I turn around and head off.

He yells, "It was good running into you this morning."

I yell back, "Likewise," with a huge grin plastered on my face.

Back at my loft, I rip my sweaty clothes off and hop into my spacious shower. This loft originally belonged to Jason, but he and my sister decided to renovate my childhood home to accommodate their new family after they got married.

I'm glad I decided to move in here; even though I enjoyed rooming with Dianella, it was time for me to find myself and learn how to live by myself. I always lived with someone else, not really taking care of myself but depending on others to get me through.

Not anymore.

I let the hot water run through my thick curly hair and slide down my body. The second the water hits my hair, it curls right up with full soft curls. I get my hair from my mom. She always had beautiful full strands flowing down her back. I miss her so much, but I have to understand that she will always be with me no matter what, just in a different way. I grab the shampoo and lather it in my hair. My mind drifts to the glorious god that saved me from breaking my ankle or, worse, knocking myself out on the concrete ground.

It felt so good being in his strong arms, smelling his manly scent all over me. Getting aroused by the remembrance of his voice saying my name, I reach down and pleasure myself. I softly rub my clit and imagine his fingers milking my pleasure. I wonder how he would feel inside of me, not knowing how a man would feel anyway. I pride myself in wanting to save myself for that special someone, but damn, I would bend over and let that sexy creature fuck me into the following week. Instead, I continue the soft assault to myself and bring an intense feeling I've felt before. My heart starts to race, and I feel a delicate silky essence run down my fingers and slide down my legs. My breath catches at the pleasure, and I let the hot water wash me off, while I continue to wash my hair and clean my body like I didn't just masturbate to the image of the sexiest man alive, Bradley Philips

Feeling refreshed and renewed.

I step out of the shower and grab my towel off the wooden towel rack. I look into the full-length mirror. I see the fainting scars left on my body from the accident. I brush my fingertips over them, remembering the excruciating pain I was in when I first received them. These scars remind me every day of what I came from and what I have today. I was told that I was fortunate to have survived that crash. My parents didn't have the same fate as me, though.

Pushing those memories to the side, I start combing through my wet strands. "I think I'm going to wear my hair curly today," I tell myself.

It's been a long time since I've worn my hair like this. After styling my hair, I put on eyeliner to enhance my features. I think my eyes are my most significant asset. After that, I brush my teeth and put on lip gloss. I don't like wearing a whole lot of makeup. It makes most women look fake.

Not the look I'm going for.

I then walk into my large walk-in closet to find something to wear. I think I want to wear a lovely short sundress to show off my legs but be relaxed at the same time. Savannah heat ain't no joke this time of

9

year. It sometimes gets up to a hundred-ten heat index. I find a white linen sundress with soft pink flowers. My sister gave this dress to me. She said it was our mother's, and she thought it would be perfect with my complexion.

I get dressed and look in the mirror for approval. "Amelia, you sure do clean up well." I grab my bag with my schoolbooks, phone, and keys. I set the alarm and head for my car. I decided to trade my car in and get myself a S500 Mercedes, just like Lily's but blacked out with black finishing. I get into the car and hear my phone ping with a message.

Unknown: *Hey Amelia, this is Brad. I thought I would send you a text with my number since you didn't ask for it.*

I laugh to myself because he's right. I didn't bother asking him for his number. I was too busy slobbering all over myself to care. I return the message.

Me: *Thanks, I appreciate it.*

I see the three tiny dots pop up as if he's about to respond. I wait in anticipation.

Bradley: *We should have drinks sometime.*

I start blushing at the offer.

Me: *Sure, just let me know when.*

Bradley: *How about tonight?*

Wow, that's sooner than I thought. But, shoot, I have dance tonight.

Me: *I have dance class tonight.*

Me: *What about tomorrow night?*

Bradley: *Sounds like a date.*

I light up with joy because I just agreed to have a date with the hottest guy in the world.

Panic seeps in through my flesh because I never been on a date.

My breathing becomes erratically fast.

And what if he's taken already? I never asked. He does have a kid.

Can I be that person?

Can I seriously be with someone who possibly goes home to another woman? Hell, no. I'm better than that.

I never even ask about Annabelle's mother. Shit, what should I do? Dianella would know what to do. I then put my phone away and head to work, more so now to talk with Dianella about this situation than actually working.

CHAPTER 2

BRADLEY

*A*nnabelle always loves it when I take her to the park. She seems happier when she spends time with me. I'm glad I decided to move to Savannah. A fresh start will give me a chance to make something out of myself while taking care of my pride and joy.

I loved her mother, but she isn't well. So when she tried to hurt Annabelle, I knew I had to do something. Annabelle is all I have besides my mother.

I could no longer take care of my mother on my own, so I had to leave her in Jacksonville, Fl, at the Mayo Clinic. She really didn't give me a choice in the matter. She didn't want to be a burden on me, so she made me promise to leave her there and focus on Annabelle. Of course, I visit every chance I get, but I have to face reality; my mother isn't getting any better and it absolutely kills me seeing the strongest person I know suffer.

I put Annabelle down for a quick nap, and then I head to the bathroom to take a shower. I commend all the single mothers out there. Taking care of a child on your own isn't easy by any means.

Sometimes, taking care of a child is more challenging than being a cop in Jacksonville. Straight out of the academy, I went into narcotics. They said they needed someone fresh and new who wasn't burnt as a cop.

Being undercover for so long started to change who I was, who I wanted to be. I was becoming the very person my mother tried so hard to keep me from. So, when I got the opportunity to get out, I did. I was able to bring down an entire cartel of drug trafficking and human trafficking.

I had the opportunity to go back in the field, but I no longer desire to be a cop. I saw some things that I wasn't proud of nor wanted to be a part of within the department. And I've heard that there are people still looking for me. So, when Mr. Ryan offered a great opportunity, I jumped at the bit.

I have a nice townhome that my boss, Mr. Ryan, lets me lease until I find something a little bigger and permanent. He offered to help, but I refused, wanting to do it independently. So a two-bedroom open concept townhome is just enough for Annabelle and me to live in for now.

I put the water on lukewarm and take off my jogging clothes. I step in the shower and let the water wash all the sweat off me.

My mind drifting to Amelia.

The first time I saw Amelia, I had to know her. She was sweet, reticent, and shy. I never pushed because I have priorities now, and I'm sure she wasn't interested in a guy with baby mama drama. She's much too good for that. She has these gorgeous hazel eyes with long wavy hair, and I can tell it wasn't fake. Most girls that throw themselves at me always have that fake shit in their heads. She's not too skinny and not too fat. She's just right with solid calves, a nice ass, and a set of tits that needs to be explored, desired. I want a real woman with natural hair and real curves. Amelia has all of those features and then some.

My ex fooled me into thinking she was the total package. Don't get me wrong, my ex is beautiful, but only when she puts all that stuff on her face, in her hair, and in her breast. I don't understand the need to change your appearance completely. I won't make that mistake again.

When I saw Amelia running in the park today, I knew it was fate. I somehow had to get her attention. But to my advantage, I didn't have to do anything at all. She was in her own world, carefree and determined; she didn't even see me in front of her.

Feeling her soft skin against my calloused fingers and smelling her alluring scent, I wanted to bend her over right then and there. But instead, I held my composure and got those digits this time. I wasn't letting her go this time.

I lather my loofa with my body wash and cleanse myself. I'm glad she agreed to have drinks with me. I really thought she would say no. I have way too much drama in my life, but it's time to move forward, not backward.

After cleaning my body, I step out of the shower. My bathroom is not that big, but it's perfect for me. It has granite countertops with a single sink. There is only a shower with no tub. There's a wall-to-wall mirror with a bay window perpendicular to the mirror. I stand in front of the mirror on heated tiles and observe the man I've become. I ask myself, am I the man my mother would approve of? Will I make her proud of me?

I hate that she will not be here to see Annabelle grow up, have her first steps, go on her first date or watch her walk across the stage. I hate that my mother has to suffer. She's all I have. My dad left when I was a young boy. He had eyes for other women and never really respected my mother. One day she caught him sleeping with another woman in their bed, and it took the grace of God not to kill both of them. Yet, I admire her for her strength and determination to move forward and never look back.

I lather my face with shaving cream and begin to shave. I prefer a clean-shaven face and a low haircut. These young boys these days like all that nappy shit on their heads. I can't stand it. I pray my daughter never brings a guy to my house with his pants hanging off his ass, gold teeth, and an IQ of shit.

Once I've completely shaved, I brush my teeth and put on some deodorant. I step out of the bathroom and enter my walk-in closet adjacent to my bathroom. It's not a super large closet, but it holds all my things. I pull out a blue suit, a pink button-down shirt, and a pink and blue tie. I pull out my peanut butter Cole Haans and my pink and blue Peppa Pig socks. One thing about it, I will be sharp when going to work. The way a man carries himself tells a lot about their character. I won't be mistaken as a thug in these streets. I will demand respect.

While getting dressed, my phone pings.

Tyra: *Where are you?*

Shit, it's Tyra. I knew this day would come; I just didn't expect it this soon. Why the fuck isn't she still in the mental Institute?

Tyra: *Answer me, Brad…*

I don't have time for this right now. I finish getting dressed. I hear the doorbell ring. While answering it, my phone pings five more times, so I turn the volume off. I open the door and find Annabelle's sitter, Daphne, standing at the door.

"Good morning Mr. Brad."

"Good morning Daphne. How are you?"

"I'm doing well. Annabelle sleeping?"

"Yes, she is. You can wake her up. We went to the park and played on the swings, so she was exhausted when we returned. Also, there are snacks, lunch, and dinner in the fridge just in case I run a little late from work."

"Thanks, Mr. Brad. Annabelle will be in great hands."

"I know. I will see you later. My cell and office numbers are on the fridge if you need anything."

"Have a good day, Mr. Brad."

"You too."

~

Driving in my black-on-black Infiniti QX80, I pull up to the firm. It's my first day working with clients since I've been here. Mr. Ryan has been teaching me everything he knows about finances, stocks and bonds, and investments. He also gave me a full scholarship to finish school. He has done so much for me; I don't want to let him down.

I take a deep breath and step out of the SUV. "You can do this," encouraging myself. I walk up to the front door and open it. I walk in with a whole new look on life.

"Good morning Mr. Philips."

I smile, "Good morning, Mrs. Megan." She gets up from behind the desk and guides me to my new office.

"You will be working in this office. I've placed some files on your desk to get you started. I will also be hiring another assistant to help you out with day-to-day stuff. But, for now, I will be assisting you with whatever you need."

"Okay, thank you, Mrs. Megan. I really do appreciate it. Is Mr. Ryan in?"

"He'll be coming in a little late. He and his wife, Mrs. Kim, has an appointment with the gynecologist. They find out the sex of the baby today."

"That's great."

"Yes, a true blessing. For now, if you need me to order anything for your office, such as furniture or supplies, just let me know. I will take care of everything. By the way, how is Annabelle? When are you going to bring her in to see me?"

"Oh, uh, I never thought about it. I just hired a full-time sitter for when I work."

"And? You can bring her anytime. This is a family business. We have a room for children to play in if you ever need her to come to work with you. We believe in family first."

"Thank you, Mrs. Megan. I will definitely keep that in mind."

"And, Mr. Ryan wants you working part-time so you can spend time with your little one. He will not take no for an answer. You'll be compensated the same."

"I—I don't know what to say."

"Say, you will bring Annabelle to see us soon. Very soon."

"Absolutely." She lights up with a smile on her face and heads out. I don't know how I became so lucky helping Mr. Ryan out that day, but as my mother always say, things always happen for a reason. She was definitely right about that.

I have a lot to be thankful for. First, I have a roof over my head and my daughter's head. Second, I can put food on the table and finishing up my degree. And best of all, I have full custody of my daughter. I'm a blessed man.

I start to sift through my papers when I hear my phone vibrating. I pick the phone up, and I have over 50 messages and 100 missed calls from none other than Tyra. I need to face her sooner than later, but I really don't need the drama today. I have work to do. Besides, if she really cared about Annabelle, she wouldn't have tried to kill her. She should have started her medication like the doctor said so many times. But, instead, she refused; therefore, I had to do what was best for Annabelle. I needed to take her out of that environment. Take her away from that woman.

I swift through my messages and see one from Amelia.

Amelia: *Hi Bradley, where are we meeting for drinks tomorrow?*

Me: *There's a nice quiet lounge on Bay Street. I think it's called the Roof Top.*

Amelia: *I know it well. I will see you around 8ish?*

Me: *I can swing by and pick you up; I don't mind at all.*

Amelia: *I actually live downtown, so if you want to park at my house and we walk, that would be okay as well.*

Me: *Cool, sounds like a plan.*

Amelia: *See you tomorrow. I will send you my address tomorrow.*

I think this can be an excellent beginning. I just hope she accepts all of me and my skeletons in the closet.

CHAPTER 3

TYRA

"Tyra, you have visitors today," the nurse announces.

"Tyra, are you going to answer the sweet lady?" the voice asks.

"Not really. I'm busy," I respond, glancing out my one window in this pathetic dump.

"What did you say, Tyra?" the nurse asks.

"Nothing. Just bring them in," I snap.

A few moments later, a tall, handsome black man and a very attractive white man walk into my room. I've never seen them before, but I wouldn't mind the entertainment.

"What can I do for the both of you?" I ask with my best seductive voice.

"Hello, Tyra. My name is Luke, and this is Dante. We have a proposition for you."

Capturing my attention, "I'm listening."

CHAPTER 4

AMELIA

"Dianella, I need your help," I announce the second I walk into the shop. I grab Dianella by the hand and pull her to an empty table.

"Maggie, can you watch the counter, please? Amelia and I have some things to discuss."

"Sure thing, hey Amelia," Maggie waves to me.

"Hi, Maggie," I respond, turning my focus back to Dianella.

"So, what's so urgent?"

I take a deep breath and begin. "Bradley asked me out on a date, and I have no idea what to do. I so need your help. What if he doesn't like me? What if I can't do this? Ugg, I'm so confused," I ramble on with frustration in my tone.

She places her hands on my shoulders. "First, you need to breathe and calm the hell down. It's a first date, not marriage. Second, I got you, sweetie. You know I'm your girl." I take a much-needed breath and calm down a little. "Is this the same Bradley that works for Ryan?"

"Yes!"

"He wouldn't have asked if he wasn't interested, so get that thought out of your head. Second, it's drinks. You will do fine. Where's he taking you?" she asks.

"He wants to go to the Rocks on the Roof."

"Excellent choice. This means he wants to get to know you better, which will give you a chance to get to know him. It's nice and cozy and quaint. Perfect for the first date. Is he picking you up?"

"Well, I offered him to park at my loft, and we could walk to the lounge. That didn't make me seem desperate, did it? Oh, gosh, I should've allowed him to pick me up."

"Stop it, Amelia, that was a good suggestion. Look, Amelia, you don't have to do anything you're not comfortable with. This is your decision. Okay?"

"Yes, I understand, but...."

"But, what?"

"Well... I've been fantasying about him."

"Really? Spill!" Dianella is definitely intrigued now.

I lower my voice because I don't want anyone else to hear. "Well, I've been imagining him touching me and pleasing me. Is that weird?"

"Of course not. We've all done it. Hell, we all still do it. That doesn't mean you have to jump into bed with him. Give it a couple of dates. Feel him out. Everyone has a story to tell. See what his story is, first. He must be a good guy for Ryan to go to these lengths to guide him and teach him. Get him talking about himself, okay?" I nod. "Most guys want you to do all the talking so they can continue to hide behind a façade. Don't let him. You give a little, then let him give a little. If he seems hesitant to talk about himself, leave him alone. He has something to hide."

"Got it. What should I wear?"

"You look fucking hot in anything you wear, but a nice cocktail dress with some killer heels will show your assets but keep something to the imagination."

I think to myself because I have a ton of dresses in my closet. I'm sure I can find something.

"Oh, and be yourself. Don't try to be something you're not. Because if this does work, you will have to keep up the act, and that's exhausting. Trust me, I know." We both laugh, and she gives me a hug. "You can do this. Just breathe. And if you do find yourself back at the house in a romantic setting, be sure to have condoms on hand. Don't do anything without protection and make an appointment with your gynecologist to get on birth control."

"Thanks, Dianella, you're the best," giving her a hug again.

"Anytime. And I want all the juicy gossip."

We both laugh again and head to the back. We have work to do.

Sitting on my balcony, drinking a glass of wine, I watch Savannahians come and go from tiny shops and bars along Broughton Street, even though it's late in the evening, and it's so muggy outside. I still sit and feel the fan I had installed cool me off. It sprays a light mist, and it's the best thing I've purchased in a long time.

I just finished dance class, where I released so much built-up stress. Between classes and dance, I've been stressing a lot. So, I sit here in peaceful bliss when my mind drifts to Bradley. I picture him intensely penetrating me with his stare. He doesn't show me that he's cruel but kind. His eyes have a hue so softly grey that they could have been drawn with a pencil. He has relaxing, purposeful, and at ease eyes.

He has a strong jawline that directly contradicts his eyes; nonetheless, I find him alluring. His chiseled arms wrap around my waist and lift me up like I weigh nothing more than a dove feather. He carries me to my bedroom and places me gently on the bed. He lifts one arm at a time and removes my sundress. He absorbs my beauty and my beastly scars with lustful eyes. Finally, he bends over, and…

Pop, Pop, Pop

Bang, Bang

The sounds jerk me out of my fantasy, and I drop to the ground of my balcony. Gunshots are ringing, and screams are echoing throughout the downtown area. I see four guys shooting at each other right under my balcony through the cracks of the wooden boards. They're all black except for one guy. It appears that there are two against two. On the west side, they both are black with hoodies and torn-up jeans. They both have black pistols in their hands, but they both suddenly drop to the ground after the guys on the east side of the sidewalk shoot at them. These guys are more open with nothing covering them up. The white guy has tattoos all over him with messy hair. He's wearing a white t-shirt and black jeans. The other black guy is tall with a cream-colored shirt and light blue jeans. He's cleaned shaven. They both are carrying guns as well.

They both take off, running down the street and duck off where I can't see them. I search everywhere for my phone. Once I find it, I dial 9-1-1.

It rings, and it rings, and it rings. "Shit, what the fuck is taking them so long to answer."

On the fifth ring, someone finally answers. "911, what is your emergency?"

"Yes, thank God. I just watched two guys shoot two other guys."

"Are you in a safe area?" the dispatcher asks.

"Yes, I'm on my balcony. I think they're gone." I get up and run into the house to put on some shoes. I still have the phone to my ear. I grab my air pods so I can be hands-free. And I grab my emergency supply bag.

"I'm headed downstairs to see if they're okay."

"Ma'am, don't do that. I need you to stay in your house until help comes."

"I can't let them die. I'm in nursing school. I can at least put pressure on the wound to stop the bleeding."

"Ma'am…"

"Please, if you're not going to help me, then I'll just hang up."

"Okay, what's your name, and where are you?"

"My name is Amelia Matthews. My sister and brother-in-law are both cops. I live on Broughton St. at Barnard St. Please hurry." I run downstairs in record time. I find the two guys on the sidewalk where they were left to die.

People are either fleeing the area or standing around live streaming. No one is trying to help. I can't believe how selfish people are or even inconsiderate.

I bend down on my knees and pull out two tourniquets. I check their pulses because they appear to be unconscious. I couldn't find a pulse for one of the guys, so I check the other. He has a faint pulse, so I place the tourniquet on his wound to stop the bleeding, and then I start CPR.

"Come on, please stay with me. I will not let you die like this… not like this." I hear sirens in the distance, and I continue CPR. The guy starts coughing up blood.

"Yes, thank God." I turn him over on his side, so he doesn't choke and continue putting pressure on his wound.

"Can you tell me your name?"

"Mi — Mich — Michael," he answers very faintly.

"Okay, Michael, you'll be okay. The ambulance is almost here."

The police arrive and immediately draw their weapons. "Show me your hands," they demand.

I don't move because if I do, I will lose him. "I can't. If I move my hands, this man will die. So you can search me or do whatever you have to do, but I will not remove my hands."

"Amelia?" I hear someone say my name, so I look up. I search for the person calling me. It's Jason.

"Oh, thank God it's you, Jason."

"Amelia, what the fuck happened? Are you okay?"

"Yes, I'm okay. There was a shoot-out, and I saw the whole thing."

"Okay, don't say another word. I have to get you out of here," glancing around and over his shoulder.

"No, not until I know this guy is okay. His friend didn't make it, but he has a chance."

"Okay, but as soon as EMS get here, you're coming with me."

"Fine." The officers start putting up crime scene tape and talking to witnesses. "Don't bother talking to anyone. They all just stood there and watched these guys choke on their own blood and did nothing. But I guarantee they have the whole thing on their phones. What assholes!"

"Yeah, that's usually the case. No one sees anything but wants us to pull miracles out of our asses. This community is useless when it comes to coming forward with information."

"Well, I'll speak. I don't care who tries to intimidate me."

"I know. I know." The ambulance finally arrives and takes Michael to the hospital. Jason then takes me to the police station in his unmarked vehicle.

I climb into the back seat and look down at my hands. There's blood all over me. I just stare and realize this will be my life once I become a nurse; seeing blood stain my hands will be a part of my every day career. I'll be trying my best to save lives, whether they deserve it or not. Everyone should receive the same amount of care, no matter the circumstances.

Jason gets in the car and heads a couple blocks to Headquarters. He doesn't say anything to me, probably because I'm a valuable witness and don't want to seem unprofessional. I don't mind I actually welcome the silence. It gives me time to focus and calm my nerves down.

We pull up to the side entrance where the chiefs usually enter. Lily always told me about everything going on at Headquarters before she decided to take a leave of absence to care for the triplets.

Jason then gets out of the car and opens the door for me. Apparently, you can't open the back doors, even in unmarked vehicles. I step out of the car and follow him into the building. It's an old building with some upgrades, but not many. It still has the original wood panels on the lower half of the walls and the original structure. It looks like the bricks have been repainted about a hundred times over the years. There are photos lined up on the wall of previous majors, I think, dating all the way back to 1956. This police barracks is the oldest functioning structure in the United States. We take the stairs to the third floor. The elevator must be broken; I rather walk anyway. He guides me into an office that is actually set up pretty nicely. It has a cute little couch with accent chairs to give it a cozy feel. A woman must have come up with this setup. I snicker to myself.

"Here's some water. I'll be right back. Are you sure you're okay?"

"Yes, I'm sure. I'm just ready for this to be over with."

"Cool, we won't keep you long." He walks out of the room and returns moments later. He sets a recorder on the table and sits in one of the accents chairs across from me. "I have to record your statement, okay?"

"Okay, I understand."

"Okay, let's start from the beginning."

I take a deep breath, and I start from the beginning. "I was sitting on my balcony drinking a glass of wine when I heard voices. I didn't bother with it because it's Broughton Street. It's always noisy and people coming and going. So, I continued to drink my wine when my mind started drifting to other things."

There is no way I'm telling him I was fantasying about a man.

"I then heard four to five gunshots. I immediately drop to the floor, and I can see between the cracks of my balcony floorboards. I saw four men, three black guys, and one white guy. The two that were shot were wearing black hoodies, and the other two guys were dressed casually like they were enjoying the nightlife. But I can't say for sure. Once the two guys with the hoodies dropped to the ground, the other two guys, one white and one black, ran off down Barnard Street. I'm not sure if they were still in the area or not. While I was still on the phone with dispatch, my need to help kicked in, and without thinking, I ran downstairs to help save those guys. One of the guys succumbed to his injuries already, the other had a faint pulse, so I put a tourniquet on him and performed CPR. For a minute there, I thought I lost him too, but I was able to revive him and keep him from choking on his own blood until y'all arrived."

"Did you recognize any of them?" Jason jotting down every word I speak.

"I don't think so. But I wasn't trying to see if I knew them or not. I know I never saw the two that ran off before, and if I saw them again, I could identify them."

"That's perfect. I'll set up a photo lineup and come back in to try to identify them. In the meantime, I need you to describe the two shooters that ran off to our sketch artist. Are you up for that? I know it's late. We just want to have as much detail as possible."

"No, I get it. I will try to help as much as possible."

"Okay. Stay here. He was called in, so it will be another fifteen minutes for him to be ready. Is there anything else I can get you?"

"No, I'm fine."

"Okay, I'll be right back."

I sit looking around and see a picture of Ryan and a picture of Lily, Jason, and the triplets. This must be Kim's office. And just like that, she comes strolling into the office with a plump belly. She should be about six months pregnant from Ryan. She's absolutely glowing.

"Oh my gosh, Amelia, are you okay? Where are you hurt? Who the fuck did this? Do I need to kick someone's ass?"

"Calm down. I'm fine, and you aren't kicking anyone's ass while pregnant, so sit down."

Taking a seat, she begins to breathe in and out slowly out her mouth. "Are you okay? That's the better question. You shouldn't be getting all worked up like this. I'm fine."

"Well, when my best friend is involved in a shooting, I have every right to be worked the hell up. Geez. Anyway, Junior here is kicking the shit out of me."

"What!!! it's a boy?" I shout with enthusiasm in my voice.

"Oh, yes. We found out earlier today. I'm convinced he will be a soccer player," she laughs out.

"Ahhh, I'm so happy. But we really need another girl to even the score. We can't let the boys take over."

"Yeah, you got that right, but it won't be coming from this coochie. If I'm in pain now, I can only imagine what the birth will be like. Ugh," she complains.

"Don't want to know. You have fun with that." We both burst out laughing when someone steps into the office.

"Hey, Frazier. How's it going?" Kim greets.

"Good, and you? I see you are expecting big things."

"What are you trying to say?"

"Uh, uh…"

Kim burst out laughing, "I'm fucking with you. Yes, three more months, and I drop the load."

"Whew, I thought I put my foot in my mouth. Congratulations."

"Thanks."

"Ms. Matthews, are you ready?"

"Oh, yes. I'm ready."

"Perfect, you can follow me. I'm Frazier, by the way. I will be conducting the sketch. Is there anything I can get you before we start?"

"Oh, no. I'm fine."

He guides me to another office, but this one is more stern and dull. It has no personality at all, with plain white walls, an easel in the middle of the room, with two hard metal chairs. There's a desk in the corner with several completed sketches.

Wow, he's really good. They look so realistic.

"Good. You can have a seat here and describe each person, including their features and build. Things like that."

"Okay. I will try my best." I begin to describe each of the men as I take a seat on one of the metal chairs.

He was done after about two hours, and I have to give it to myself and Mr. Frazier; the sketches looked exactly like the men.

No thanks to my ass bone. Geez, my ass hurts like hell from sitting down way too long.

"That's amazing. I've heard of these types of identifications, but this is way beyond my belief. I feel I'm standing at the crime scene all over again staring at the men who killed that guy."

"Thank you. I certainly try. I give the credit all to you. Your attention to detail is impeccable. I can't do what I do without the help of people like you, so thanks."

"Of course, what happens now?"

"Well, I scan the sketch into the system and run it through all of our databases. So if they're in there, we will get a hit."

"Cool, can I watch?"

"Uh, I'm not sure. I have to ask Detective Hall. He's the lead on the case. So it will be up to him."

"Oh, okay. No need. I don't want to be a bother. I just like learning new things."

"Okay, well, we're done here, so you can head back to Detective Knight's office. Do you remember where that is?"

"Uh, yes, I think I can find my way. Thank you for all your help. I appreciate it."

"Of course, it's my job." I then head back to Kim's office.

"Hi, Kim."

"Hey, once I'm done running this information. I can take you home. It will take about thirty minutes. Is that okay with you?"

"Yes, of course. Take all the time you need." I sit back and watch her in action. I find it fascinating how she can find anything through the internet. All she needs is a name and a date of birth. Sometimes she needs less than that. I wonder if she can look up Bradley.

No Amelia. Stop it. That's crazy. You are not a stalker.

"Earth to Amelia." I snap out of my head and look at Kim staring at me. "Where were you?"

"What do you mean?"

"I was talking to you, and you didn't hear a word I said."

"Just thinking."

"About?"

"Well, I have a date tomorrow with Bradley, but now I think I need to call it off."

"You won't do no such thing. Don't let him suffer because of what happened tonight. It's not fair to him. Besides, he seems like a pretty good guy. I feel bad for what he's going through, but overall, he's a pretty decent person."

Piquing my interest, "What do you mean, going through something?"

"Shit, I said too much. It's his story to tell, not mine," avoiding my piercing gaze.

"Oh, come on," I whine. "You can't say something like that and not give me something. Please. Pretty please with a cherry on top."

"Oh, cut it out. Okay, I'll tell you a little. The rest, you shall get from him."

"Deal," waiting in anticipation on the edge of my seat.

"Well, you know he has a daughter, right?" I node my head urging her to go on. "Well, her mother is bipolar and schizophrenic. She refuses to take her medication, so she has multiple episodes and cannot control them. Brad left her when she tried to drown their daughter in the bathtub. She kept saying that she was evil and dirty and needed to be cleansed. After that, Brad got full custody of his daughter and hasn't allowed the mother to see her since. The report states that he's afraid that she may do something to their daughter."

"Oh my gosh, that's awful. I knew something was off, but I had no idea it was that."

"There's more, but please, let him tell you."

"Shit, there's more? That little bit is just enough; who can do more than that to their daughter?"

"You would be amazed at what people are capable of when they're mentally ill."

"Yeah, I see. I learn about it in school, but I've never really experienced it, well, except for the guys trying to kill Lily and your mom and dad selling you to the highest bidder. There are some really sick people out there."

"You got that right. Ah-ha! Got a match on both sketches. Now, playtime," she rubs her hands together. Within minutes, she had their entire background history from the day they were born and beyond that. I've never seen anything like it.

Once she was done, she handed over all the information to Jason. "All done, boss. I'll take Amelia home."

"Amelia, are you sure you'll be, okay? You can always stay with us," Jason suggests.

"No, I'll be fine. Besides, I don't want to be a bother."

"You're family. We take care of each other."

"Thanks for the offer, but I just want to take a shower and get into my own bed."

"Okay, but if you need anything, please let us know."

"Okay."

Kim and I leave headquarter and head to my loft. Suddenly, exhaustion spreads over me, and I just want to lay down and go to sleep. It's been a long day. Kim pulls into the garage and lets me out.

"Amelia, if you need anything, call Jason or me. We'll be here before you know it. I also placed your home on extra patrol just in case."

"Okay, thanks, Kim. I appreciate everything."

"I'll call Dianella and let her know what happened. You stay home and get rest and go on that date."

"Okay, okay. I will."

She then drives away, and I take the elevator to my loft.

CHAPTER 5

BRADLEY

*I*t's early in the morning, and I can't sleep. So, I head into the kitchen and make myself a cup of coffee and turn on the news. The news is always depressing, but I must keep up with current events as they sway the financial market.

Apparently, according to the news, there was a shooting downtown. One victim succumbs to their injuries while the other is in critical condition. The police are asking for any information involving the tragedy.

Man, no matter where you go, there's crime. I really don't understand the need to take someone else's life for no reason. These thugs need to work for what they want instead of taking from people who work hard. I think very low of a person who takes another's life because of stupidity. Hopefully, this shooting was justified, but I'm pretty sure it wasn't.

I pour creamer into my coffee and take a slip. Just as I drink my coffee, I spit it everywhere. I look closely at the news of the scene last night, and I see Amelia standing over a body.

"What the fuck?" I grab my phone prepared to call her but realize it's five in the morning. "Shit. Think." I then send her a text.

Me: *Are you okay? I saw the news.*

I hold the phone in anticipation of her response. Not even seconds later, she responds.

Amelia: *Yes, I'm okay. Just a little shaken up. Other than that, I'm fine.*

Me: *Are you sure? It's okay to talk about it.*

Amelia: *We can actually talk about it during our date?*

Me: *Are you sure you still want to go out?*

Amelia: *Absolutely. I need to get out. I'm already taking the day off since I literally just got home.*

Me: *Wow, you've been up all night?*

I figured they would keep her. She's a key witness to a homicide.

Amelia: *Yeah, I was headed to sleep when I heard my phone ping.*

Me: *You could have ignored it.*

Amelia: *And let you suffer all day…*

Me: *Lol, yeah, I actually take that back.*

Amelia: *I figured.*

Me: *See you tonight. Get some rest.*

Amelia: *Okay, by the way, my address is 220 Broughton Street.*

Me: *Thanks, good night.*

Amelia: *Yw, good morning.*

I shake my head, wondering how she can be so calm about what she experienced. But then again, she's going to school for nursing. So, she probably seen worse than that. She literally lives in the area where the shooting occurred; no wonder they brought her in for questioning. I just hope she's okay. I need to make sure our date is as stress-free as possible tonight.

I head into Annabelle's room to check on her. She's ordinarily awake about this time. I walk into the room, and I hear her cooing to herself. She's reaching up to play with the stuffed animals hanging above her. She's really growing up. I watch her for a while before I disturb her. Once she sees me, she gives me the biggest wet smile in the world. She's so perfect. Anyone who comes in contact with her falls in love immediately, well, except one person.

I pick her up and head to the kitchen to make her breakfast. She loves bananas and strawberries. I sit her in her highchair when my phone pings with a message.

Tyra: *You can't keep Annabelle from me.*

Me: *Actually, I can, and I will. You need help.*

Tyra: *Fuck you, Brad. I want my daughter.*

Me: *When you prove to your doctors and me that you're okay, we can discuss visitation. Until then, you will not come near her.*

And I mute my phone from receiving messages. I really need to get another phone. She's aggravating as hell. I can't believe I used to be in love with someone like that, but she was much different than she is now. She was sweet and pleasant to be around. She was nothing like she is now. I really tried to stick around, but I had to protect my baby girl. I can't let her go through that again. A mother could want to protect her child, not harm her.

I continue to feed Annabelle and then clean her up.

"Do you want to go to the park this morning? It's a beautiful morning to play on the swings." She claps her tiny hands together like she understands what I'm saying.

"That must mean a yes." I change her clothes and get myself dressed. I put her in her stroller, and we head to the park.

It's a beautiful day with the sun shining and the breeze flowing. I love the downtown area because it's cozy and quaint, and for the most part, all my neighbors are welcoming. I'm going to miss them when I eventually move.

I cross Whittaker Street and head towards the swings. Annabelle loves flying in the air. She's so full of life, and she rarely cries. However, there were two times when Annabelle really was scared, the incident with her mother and a woman came up to her and tried to touch her face. One thing about it Annabelle will tell me when she doesn't like a person.

I pick her up and place her in the swing and wrap her tiny hands around the chains holding the swing up. I then get in front of her so she can see me and push her gently. Then, she starts laughing and wants to go a little higher. So, I push her a little harder.

"Hi," a woman says as she approaches with her daughter.

"Hey."

"Can we join you?" she asks.

"Sure, plenty of room for everyone." I continue to push my daughter because I really don't want to be bothered. This is my time with my baby girl. And I have to cautious at all times. The people I were dealing with in Jacksonville want me dead for betraying them.

"I've seen you out here a couple of times. Do you live in the area?" she asks. So much for peace and quiet.

"Yeah, just across the way."

"Oh, okay. My name is Claire," showing all twenty-six teeth and flinging her hair countless times over her shoulder.

I would be rude if I just ignored her, but I don't want to make enemies in this neighborhood.

"Brad. Nice to meet you." Obviously, she is trying to flirt with me but hasn't received the hint that I'm not interested. Don't get me wrong, she's an attractive woman, pale skin, long dark hair pulled into a ponytail, and green eyes. But she's just not for me. Those days of sleeping around with random women are over. I got it out of my system once I moved here. I have one woman on my mind.

She continues her interrogation. "Are you from Savannah?"

"No, I'm from Jacksonville. I got a job opportunity here, so I packed up and moved without looking back."

"Wow, that's incredible. I've lived in Savannah, all my life. I probably will never leave."

I continue to push Annabelle on the swing, making her laugh and giggle.

"You have such a beautiful little girl. If you ever need a playdate, we live on Drayton Street side."

"I will keep that in mind. Thank you."

"Anytime." That is my moment to leave.

"Come, baby girl. It's time to go inside. Daddy has to get ready for work."

"Oh, you're leaving so soon?"

"Yeah, I have work to do. See you later."

"I hope so." She flashes a smile at me, and I grin, turn away and walk off with my baby girl in her stroller.

I'm sitting in my office, completely decorated with refurbished wood, washed with white accents. I didn't want dark furniture. I tried to liven the mood during meetings. There's a distressed conference table in the Northeast corner of the room that sits eight for times I'm closing on deals. My desk sits in the middle of the room with book-shelves lining the wall behind me. Mrs. Megan places a nice wet bar fully stocked with Ghost Coast whiskey and rum, a local brand mad just off of Indian St. She chose different historical landscapes from right here is Savannah. She done good; real good.

Mrs. Megan walks into my office.

"Mr. Bradley, how do you like the office?"

"It looks good. Thank you. I like the paintings you picked out. Different landscapes with blues and greens really set off the color scheme."

"I'm glad you like it. By the way, I'm holding interviews for your assistant today. Would you like to sit in?"

"Sure, I just need to finish up on a couple of files, and I will be right in. When will Mr. Ryan return?"

"He will be back next week."

"Okay." She walks out, and I finish looking over my files. After about twenty minutes, I take a break and join Mrs. Megan for the interviews. I missed the first interview, but I wanted to stick my head in for the second one. Once I walked in, it's no other than Claire from the park. I had to do a double-take.

"Brad? Is that you?" Shit, she noticed me before I could walk out.

"You know Mr. Philips?" Mrs. Megan asks her.

"Yes, I've seen him at the park with his daughter. We live in the same neighborhood. What a small world," Claire beams.

"Yes, small indeed," I respond flatly. "Mrs. Megan, I have more files to take care of. Once you're done, please meet me in the office."

"Yes, sir," catching the hint I didn't want to be in there. So I head back to my office and returned some calls.

About an hour later, Mrs. Megan walks through the door.

"Hi, Mr. Bradley. What was that?"

"She lives in my neighborhood. She was trying to come on to me at the park, but I left her standing there."

"I can always deny her application."

"No, no, no, be fair. I don't want her thinking we weren't fair about the hiring process."

"You're a good person."

"I try."

I left work a little early to get ready for my date with Amelia. I've been waiting for this moment for all day.

I asked the sitter if she could stay longer tonight to watch Annabelle for a couple of hours. While Annabelle is sleeping, I take a shower and get ready. I've decided to wear jeans, a button-down blue shirt, and a Linen sports coat. I check myself in the mirror and then get ready to head out.

"Daphne, I appreciate you staying a little later tonight. Your parents don't mind?"

"No, sir, it's summer break, so they're fine with it."

"Okay, if you need anything, my number is on the fridge."

"I know Mr. Brad. Go have fun. Annabelle will be okay."

Chuckling, "I know."

I then walked out of the house, get in the car, and head to Amelia's house.

I pull into the private garage of Amelia's home. "Wow, this place is nice from the outside, I can only imagine what it looks like inside. I was not expecting this." I park the car and then take the elevator to her loft. I ring her doorbell and wait for her to open the door. I then hear the door open, and before my eyes, the most beautiful woman stands in front of me in a fantastic dress. I just stand there speechless because I've never seen anything remotely close to this type of beauty. Her eyes alone are hypnotizing, and that long hair. I just want to run my fingers through her long thick strands. She has an ass of a goddess and hips thick, just the way I like it. She's wearing this sexy green dress that flows just above her knees. I can only imagine what she's wearing underneath. Jesus, I'm getting hard as a rod just thinking about it. I need to control myself. It's been a long time since I've been with someone.

"Hi, Bradley."

"Uh, hi Amelia, you look breathtaking."

"Thank you. You don't look half bad yourself."

"Are you ready to head out?"

"Yes, here, let me turn off all the lights and set the alarm. You can come in if you like."

I step into her home, and I'm mesmerized at how beautiful her home is. This is what I'm working towards. A home like this for Annabelle and me. "Your home is beautiful."

"Thank you. It was my brother-in-law's. Once he and my sister got married, they moved into my childhood home, and I moved in here to give them privacy. We wanted to keep the loft in the family."

"I don't blame you. Once I get acclimated to the area, I want to look for something like this for Annabelle and me."

"That's great. Once you start, get with Ryan. He has a lot of connections and can find you a diamond in the rough. Trust me."

"I sure will."

"How is Annabelle anyway? I miss her already. She's so adorable."

"She's doing fine. Getting used to the change and all."

"People don't realize that change can affect children just as much as adults. I'm glad she's adjusting well. I would love to spend time with her if that's okay with you?"

Setting the alarm and turning off all the lights, we step out of the loft. "That would be great. I think she likes you."

"Of course, she does. I'm a likable person." That you are. I say to myself; likable and fuckable.

We head down the elevator and reach the sidewalk. It's a nice night to walk. I'm glad she suggested it.

"It's a gorgeous night," she says.

"Yes, it is. Unfortunately, I'm so busy at work I barely have time to enjoy the scenery. But, I know there's so much history here to explore."

"Well, if you ever need a tour guide, I'm your girl. I love history and learning new things."

"Bet, sounds good to me."

We're walking through City Market, and people are hopping from one bar to the next, people chilling in Ellis Square, and bands playing live music.

"So, tell me something about yourself," Amelia insists, locking her fingers in mine. Here we go with the questions, but I don't mind answering them for the first time. Just the simple gesture of holding hands gives me life.

"Well, I was born and raised in Jacksonville, Florida. This is the first time I've ever left to explore better opportunities. How about you?"

"I've lived here all my life. It's great that you can be able to relocate. Some people find it difficult."

"Yeah, it was difficult, and there are still times where I think I made a mistake, but for the most part, I'm glad I made the leap."

"I'm glad you did as well. What about your parents?"

"I never met my dad, and my mother is my life, besides Annabelle. I had to leave her in Jacksonville because she suffers from stage four breast cancer, and it doesn't look good. She made me promise to leave her there and live my dream and take care of Annabelle. It was the hardest thing I had to do, but I have to accept that there is nothing more I can do for her but go visit as often as I can."

"Wow, I'm sorry to hear that. I know all too well the loss of a parent. It's tough."

"Oh, I'm sorry. I didn't know."

"It's okay. It's been a long time now. I lost my parents in a car accident and almost lost my sister. Lily, my sister, raised me and made sure I was taken care of when our parents died. As a matter of fact, they died on my sixteenth birthday, and I was placed in foster care until Lily won full custody of me. She was only nineteen and had to take care of a physically injured and emotionally distraught teenager."

"What do you mean you were injured?"

"I was in the car as well during the accident. Both my legs were broken, and I had internal bleeding. My sister was in Atlanta going to school at the time. She dropped out to take care of me."

Holy shit. I had no idea. "Wow, that's rough."

"For a while, it was. But we're doing as well as come be now, well besides the time my sister was kidnapped by the very people who killed our parents and our best friend being sold through sex trafficking. Trust me, my family has been through some shit, but we're troopers. I give it to us; we can handle our own."

"Are you kidding me? That's more than anyone can handle, let alone survive. And I thought I had it bad."

"Oh no. Never downplay what you've experienced in life. Everyone handles things completely different and perceives things differently.

Yeah, we've been through hell, but that experience made us who we are today."

"I guess I never thought of it that way." We're approaching the elevators to the Roof Top when she stops in front of me, tall and confident.

"I really like you, and I adore Annabelle. I'm certainly willing to try if you are. There's so much we need to know about each other, and we will as long as we're a hundred percent with each other. Okay?"

Like she was seeing straight through my soul, she took the thoughts right out of my head. "One Hundred."

She puts a beautiful smile on her face and pushes the button to head to the top. Once the elevator opens, we're the only ones who enter. So, I do something I never thought I would do. I grab her by the waist and push her up against the elevator wall. I hold both sides of her face, and I explore her lips with mine. She opens to me immediately, giving me everything I want in this kiss. Her lips are soft and smooth. She tastes of raw peaches, and I want more. I slip my tongue into her mouth, and she opens up graciously. I grind my hard dick against her pelvic bone, and I can smell her arousal. Fuck, she smells so fucking good. I swipe my tongue over her teeth and twirl it around her tongue. I want so much more; I'm practically dying of thirst. The elevator opens, and I push away, taking a much-needed breath.

Fuck, that was utterly amazing.

I could feel the tingle in my toes and fingertips as if electricity struck through my veins. She's panting as well as we step out of the elevator. Both of us speechless. I take her hand and guide her to an empty table where we can sit side-by-side. My dick still hard as a fuck.

"Holy shit. That was unbelievable," she admits between breaths. "I've never been kissed like that."

"I'm sorry if I was too forceful; I've just wanted to do that for so long now."

"I will let you know if you force me into anything. That right there was breathtaking. I'm fine. Like, better than fine."

A waitress comes up to the table to take our orders. Soft music playing from the live band, and it's not crowded at all.

"Hi, I'm Dee, and I'll be serving you tonight. What can I get you to start off?"

"Amelia?" I announce. Letting her order first.

"Can I get a mojito, please?"

"Sure can... uh hey, aren't you Jason and Ryan's sister?"

"Yes, I am."

"Okay, don't worry about the tab. Your money is no good here. Jason and Ryan have done so much for us. We want to return the favor." Wow, Ryan and Jason's name really carries around here. I don't know if I should be grateful or offended.

"Oh, you don't have to do that," Amelia pleads.

"I know, but I insist."

"Okay, well, if you insist."

"What can I get for you, sir?" Dee asks.

"It's Brad, and I'll take a Tennessee Mule," with a little more sternness than I wanted to project.

"Wow, you must be related to them too."

"Why do you say that?"

"They always order that very drink."

We all laugh. After the day I've had, I needed a good laugh. But mostly, I just want to bend Amelia over this table and fuck the shit out of her.

"So, I hate to bring this up, but where's Annabelle's mother?" And just like that, the fucking mood is lost.

45

"Well —"

"You don't have to talk about it if you don't want to," she interrupts, knowing that statement is farther from the truth.

"I really don't, but I respect you enough to tell you the truth. You need to know what you're getting yourself into." Then, after a short pause, "Tyra, Annabelle's mother, and I dated since high school. She was my first love, my everything. She was a very nice girl and would do anything for anyone, but her mood started to change after we graduated, and then she became pregnant with Annabelle. At first, I thought it was the mood swings from the pregnancy, like, what do you call it again?" drawing a blank.

"Postpartum depression?" Amelia answers.

"Yes, but once Annabelle was born, she became worse. She would yell and curse so much, and she would get upset about everything. There were times when Tyra would hit me, but I just brushed it off because I loved her, and of course, I thought it would pass. But, one day, I can home from work, and she and Annabelle were in the bathroom. The door was locked, so I knocked on the door. She started screaming that she hated our daughter and wished she was never born," taking a deep breath, Amelia grabs my hand to comfort me. It's working because I can feel myself physically calm down, not realizing I was shaking.

"I then decided to kick in the door and found her holding Annabelle under the water. I picked Tyra up off the ground and threw her as hard as possible. She slammed to the wall and went unconscious. I then picked my baby girl up out of the water." I can feel the tears running down my face. "She wasn't breathing, so I started CPR and prayed to God that she was okay. I called 911, and they talked me through everything to do for Annabelle. I could revive her, but I was scared it might be too late. If I had lost her, I don't know what I would have done. Annabelle means everything to me."

"I know Bradley, I know." I continue my story.

"After the police arrived, they took both my girls from me. Tyra was placed in a mental facility, and Annabelle was placed in foster care until I could prove that I was a fit father. It was the worst experience of my life, but I thank God that I got my baby girl back. I love Tyra, but not like I used to. I love her because she gave me my baby girl, but I can no longer be in love with her. I tried so hard to do right by her, but I cannot forgive her for what she did to Annabelle. I just can't."

"Bradley, it's okay. You did what you had to do. No one will think differently of you. I don't, and I never will. You were supposed to protect your daughter. If you didn't, who would?"

I shrug my shoulders because I feel less than a man. I'm a first date with the most beautiful girl in the world, and I'm crying like a pussy. Get your shit together, Brad.

"Like I said before, we all go through something. It's what we do after, that makes us the person we are today." I gaze out the window and watch a vast cargo ship pass by, letting my thoughts drift anywhere but this moment. "Look at me," I turn at the command. "Stop feeling sorry for yourself. We're out having a good time," she pulls me to my feet. "Dance with me."

I reluctantly follow her to the dance floor. I begin swaying to the music, trying to feel it. She then starts dancing, and it's the most angelic thing I've ever witnessed. She's smooth on her feet and flowing like a feather in the wind. She closes her eyes and falls in love with the song. She's performing as if we're the only people in the lounge. This right here is so fucking hot; I grab her by the hips and whisper in her ear. "Let's get out of here."

"Okay," she whispers back. I walk over to the table and drop a hundred-dollar bill. I can't just walk away without paying for anything. I then grab Amelia's hand and head for the elevator. I push the button impatiently as hell. She runs her small hands over the stiff muscles in my back, and just that simple touch got me wanting to fuck her. Finally, the elevator opens, and I practically dragged her inside. When the doors closed, I push her up against the wall again and devoured her mouth with mine. She tastes of peach and mint, and I want more.

The elevators open again, and I force myself to push off her once again. I practically drag her down the street because I want to feel that pussy so fucking bad. I honestly don't know how she's keeping up with my speed, but she is.

We make it to her loft in record time, and she pulls her keys out and opens the door before I can even step off the elevator. I push her inside and start kissing her like it will be the last time I will ever be able to kiss her. She tastes so good; I don't want to stop. I reach under her dress and feel her soft skin under my calloused hands.

I ask the question I always dread, but I respect her so much I don't want to mess this up. "Are you ready for this?"

"Um," she hesitates a moment, and I back off. My dick hard as fuck, "No, please, I want this, I just—I never—Um."

"You never what?" I look into her pretty deep hazel eyes, and I think I see fear in them. And finally hits me after a moment. Holy shit. "Are you a virgin?" I blurt out.

"Um, yes," she hesitantly admits.

"You've done other things, right?" She shakes her head back and forth. "How have you've waited so long?" flabbergasted by her response, where has she been all my life.

"I wanted to make love to the right person. And I haven't found him yet...well, not until now... I think."

"I've basically devoured you in the elevator twice. Shit, how did I not know this? How did I miss this?" pacing back and forth.

"It's okay, Bradley; I want to with you," stopping in my tracks, I study her eyes. Those hypnotic hazel-colored eyes, and it's the most alluring look she could ever give me. Breaking me completely down, I take her hand gently.

"Where's your bedroom?"

"Down the hall."

We enter her bedroom, and I guide her to the bed. I look into her eyes again. "Are you sure?" She nods her head. "No, I need to hear you say it."

"Yes, I'm sure. Please make love to me."

That's all I needed to hear. I lift her dress over her head and reveal a sexy white lace bra with a matching thong. I gently push her to the bed and tower over her. I take off my blazer and my button-down shirt, revealing my solid eight pack. I bend over her, kissing her neck, dragging my tongue between her breast, cupping both of them in my hands. I continue trailing my tongue down her stomach and over her naval. Finally, she begins to arch her back off the bed. I can't get enough of her.

Reaching down in between her legs, I gently pull her panties off. I inhale them, smelling all her essences from her arousal. She smells so fucking good. I then glide my tongue over her clit and suck gently. She nearly bucks off the bed, but I hold her down with my arms and continue sucking and tugging at her clit. I insert one finger at a time to get her used to feeling pleasure between her legs.

"Oh my god, Bradley. That feels so good."

"Yes, baby, I want you to come for me. Can you do that for me?"

"I think so," sounding so innocent at that moment; I forget she's a grown-ass woman. I continue my assault, wanting her to come inside my mouth, needing to taste her. I insert two more fingers, and she nearly loses her mind.

"That's it, baby; I want you to come for me." As if right on command, I feel her come inside my mouth, sucking all her essence out of her. She screams at the top of her lungs, and she's shaking uncontrollably.

"Oh, my—shit, Bradley. I—I."

"That's it, baby, give it to me." I then stand up and remove my jeans and boxers, allowing her to recover before continuing, I grab a condom out of my pocket, rip the foil and then stretch it over my dick.

"Oh my gosh, you about to put that inside of me?" I smirk a little because she's so cute right now, eyes wide as biscuits.

"It's going to hurt a little at first, but once I'm in, you'll love it."

"Okay," she responds innocently.

"I just need you to relax, okay? It's easier if you relax your muscles."

"Okay." She takes a deep breath and physically relaxes.

"That's it, baby." I then hover over her and support my weight with my arms so I don't crush her. She's so tiny. I grab the tip of my dick and gently glide it over her pussy. Fuck she feels good. I stick the head in abruptly to allow her to get over the pain quickly.

"Ouch," she screams, digging her nails into my arms. I then push further in and stretch her a little bit at a time, allowing the pain to flow down my arms from her sharp nails.

"Shit, that feels good."

"You like it, baby? I'm not hurting you, am I?"

"No, not at all. Please don't stop. I want more."

I give her what she wants and pick up the speed.

"Fuck, you feel damn good, Amelia."

"I do? Am I doing this right?" she asks.

"God, yes. You don't have to do anything; I'll do all the work. Okay?"

"Okay." I thrust into her, in and out, over and over again. I pick up the speed because this is the best pussy I've ever had. This is way better than Tyra. How the fuck did I stay with her for so long when I have this prime pussy right here.

"Fuck, Amelia. You're so tight. You're clinching me like a python about to kill its prey. I've wanted you for so long."

"I wanted you too, Bradley." God, I love the way she says my name. I thrust harder and harder. I then slow down, pulling almost entirely out, and slam back into her. I feel her clenching harder, and I know she's about to have another orgasm.

"Bradley, god, I think I'm about to come again."

"Yes, baby. That's it. Come all over this dick. This dick is yours, baby. All yours." She then clenches tighter and comes all over me. I can't hold on any longer.

"Baby, Amelia, I'm coming. Fuck, goddamnit. Amelia, I'm still coming." She holds on for dear life, as I finish. We both are sweaty and breathing hard, completely sated. I roll off of her and head to the bathroom to clean myself up. Her bathroom is fucking huge for just one person. She has a double sink vanity with a full mirror on top. Her shower is detached from her large acrylic LED water massage bathtub. I clean myself up and find a clean washcloth to clean her as well. I run warm water on the cloth and find her sprawled all over the bed with her hair flowing across the pillows. She's so beautiful. I then get in bed with her and spread her legs gently. I run the warm cloth over her, cleaning away any blood she might have spilled from the tearing. I then wrap my arms around her, spooning her closer to me.

I miss this. Lying in bed naked with someone next to me. It's been so long since I've done this I almost forget how much it means to me. I've never been an average dude. I was always on the romantic side. Doing little shit to please Tyra, and she never appreciated it. She always said she wanted a thug nigga. I was never that nor aspired to be that.

Amelia wraps my arms tighter around her as if she's enjoying this moment as well. Because we both know I have to leave and go back home.

"Thank you," Amelia whispers.

"For what?"

"For being so open with me today and being so gentle. You were the perfect gentleman, and I love that about you. You didn't make me feel less of a woman for not being experienced enough. So, thank you."

"No need to thank me. You actually did me a favor. I almost forgot what it was like to be with a woman, a real honest to god woman. That means more to me than fucking someone on the streets. So, no, thank you."

She then kisses me on my hand. "I know you have to go back home to Annabelle, but can we do this again?"

"Of course. You're stuck with me now. You're too perfect to let go."

"Do you think you can bring Annabelle next time? I'll have my nephews and niece over this weekend, and I would love for her to come over as well for a playdate. But, of course, she can bring her daddy if she wants."

We both laugh, "Absolutely. I think Annabelle would love that. She's so good with you."

"Perfect, then it's a date." I kiss her on her hair and then get out of bed. She gets up too and puts on a robe. I then put my clothes back on and glance at my watch. Good, it's not too late. After I put my clothes on, she reaches up on her tippy toes because she's so much shorter than me, and she kisses me on the lips. "Text me when you get home. I want to make sure you make it safely."

"Sure thing." I then kiss her forehead, and she walks me to the door. I turn around one last time, "I really enjoyed you tonight."

"I fucking enjoyed you too." We both laugh, and I walk out.

I feel my phone vibrating in my pocket and automatically assume it's Amelia.

Tyra: *You fucking another bitch. That's why you won't return my calls.*

Tyra: *Were you thinking of me when you came inside your tweety bird pussy?*

Tyra: *Son of a bitch, I'm coming for ya and yo tweety bird bitch.*

Fuck, it's Tyra.

CHAPTER 6

AMELIA

"*T*hat feeling you get when you're completely satisfied in every way; almost like eating salted cameral ice cream with Nothing Bundt Cakes. That's the feeling I had when Bradley made love to me last night. Oh my gosh, I never felt anything like it in my life. Why didn't you tell me it would feel this way?" I question Dianella.

Dianella and I are preparing to open the café while still thinking of the fantastic night I had with Bradley. Now that I've had a taste of what I've been missing, I don't want to let it go.

"Well, I've had sex before, several times, but never felt what you're describing with Lenny or anyone else. They say it's almost like a drug and needing your next fix."

"It's not just that. He talked me through everything he was going to do, and he made sure that I was okay and that I really wanted to do it. He was the perfect gentleman, and I can't imagine experiencing anything else."

"It's scarce to have found something so pure like that on your first time. Most people never even experience it, let alone know that it exists. You're fortunate. Did he open up to you about his past?"

"Yeah, he did. It was utterly heartbreaking. I honestly don't know how he endured so much pain without losing his mind. I'm totally astounded at his willingness to push on, let alone take the responsibility to take care of his daughter on his own. Don't get me wrong, I know there are always three sides to a story, his side, her side, and the truth, but I couldn't help but feel sympathy for his experience."

"Just be careful. I don't know of any woman in her right mind who would give up their child so easily."

"She isn't in her right mind."

"That makes it even worse. She may become resentful in her state of mind and want revenge. Just be careful."

"Okay." We both go back to cleaning up when Maggie walks through the door.

"Good morning, rays of sunshine."

"Good morning," I beam, still feeling Bradley's hands all over my body. Goosebumps scattering across my arms, shit, I need to get it together. I'm just like a horny teenager.

"Good morning, Maggie," Dianella shoots back.

What y'all bitches up too?"

We both look at each other and start giggling. "Nothing," we both announce.

"That's a load of croak. Spill the beans."

"Amelia here went on her first date last night."

"Holy shit. I want every detail," Maggie exclaims.

"Why does everyone want to know about my love life?" rolling my eyes.

"Because it's bright and shiny right now. Once you've had a few, it starts to get dull."

"Don't ever see that happening with Bradley," I defend.

"Give it a few. It's coming," Maggie says nonchalantly.

"Wow, stop feeding the poor girl your mellow dramatics. Let her experience her own love without your inputs," Dianella defends me.

"Fine, but don't come running to me when you find out the hard way."

"I'm pretty sure I won't."

We all burst out laughing. "Hey, Maggie, can you open the doors. We're ready to open." Maggie opens the doors, and two men enter, one black and one white. They're both dressed in khaki shorts and V-neck shirts. Three more couples stroll in behind them.

Holy shit, they're the guys who shot those guys the other night. I bump Dianella in the shoulder, letting her know to be alert. She looks at me with a puzzling look. I nod toward the guys and motion my hand onto a gun behind the counter.

"You can sit anywhere you like," Maggie offers. Everyone nod at her and head towards Dianella and me at the front counter.

"Can we get coffee, black, and 2 cranberry muffin tops to go, please?" the Black guy asks. They seem to not recognize me from the news.

Thank God.

"Sure thing," says Dianella. I just stand there like an idiot with my hand on the gun under the counter, ready to shoot for whatever reason.

"Is everything okay? You don't look so well," the white guy asks me.

"Uh, yes. I'm okay. Just under the weather this morning. Can we get y'all anything else?"

"No, we're good." They then walk over to the countertop to wait on their orders. The other three couples glancing through the glass of pastries and cakes.

I pull Dianella to the back. "Oh my gosh, it's them." I start pacing the hall because I'm nervous as shit, my anxiety kicking in.

"It's who, honey?"

"It's the guys who shot those guys in front of my loft."

"Are you sure?"

"Positive. I'll never forget their faces."

"Okay, take a deep breath. I'll prepare their order, and you call my brother and let him know the suspects from the shooting the other night is in the café."

"Okay," I respond, physically shaking from the anxiety.

"Amelia, you can do this." She places her hands on my shoulders centering me, and looks me in the eyes with such authority yet compassion.

"Okay." I take a deep breath and pull out my phone. Dianella heads back to the front and gives them their order. Once they leave, she shuts and locks the front door. Maggie assist the other couples while Dianella and linger in the back.

I call Jason, and he answers on the first ring. "Jason, those guys just came into the café."

"Where are they now?"

"I think they just left. Hold on a minute. I have you on speakerphone. Dianella just walked in."

"Hey, Jason. This is Dianella. I took a picture of the car they were driving in. It's a black Chevy Caprese convertible, eighties style. They just left the café and headed south on Bull Street."

"Perfect. Thanks. Keep the café closed for now. I will have forensics head over to you. Did they say anything or ask for anything?"

"No, they just wanted a cup of coffee and cranberry muffin tops."

"Okay, good. Amelia, everything will be okay. It appears that they didn't recognize you. I want to keep it that way." I listen intently like it's the last thing on earth that will save my life.

"Okay." He then hangs up.

Dianella turns to me and looks me in my eyes. I never really noticed how beautiful her eyes are. They're the color of midmorning springily green grass or a tropical forest right after a summerly shower of rain. They strike me as being willfully protective and robust.

"Amelia, everything will be okay. You did the right thing." She rubs my back and brings me in for a hug. Her touch soothes the tension in my muscles. I'm blessed to have such beautiful people in my life. I gained a great brother-in-law and a wonderful sister through my sister's marriage. I'm so glad they're in my life.

The forensics unit showed up about fifteen minutes later and dusted the countertops and the door. Maggie went to the back and continued baking for when we reopen. She didn't ask a word or say anything about what just happened. That's a little strange, but I just let it go. I sit down at one of the tables and watch the officers do their job, contemplating life in general.

How does a person decide to take another human being's life? Like, what do they think when they do decide? I understand having to defend yourself, but how do you wake up in the morning and say, 'I think I'm going to kill someone.' How? Dianella brings me a cup of coffee and a Cheese Danish.

"Why don't you take the rest of the day off. Maggie and I can handle things around here."

"No, I rather stay. If I go home, I'm just going to sit around thinking of that night or today. I need a change of pace, something to do."

"I get it. But if you change your mind, we got your back."

"Thank you. I appreciate that more than you know." Lately, I haven't been pulling my own weight around here. So I'm going to have to do something for Dianella. She has really been a godsend to me.

"I know. What are sisters for." She smiles and gets up to help Maggie in the kitchen. I hear my phone ping and look down at the screen.

Bradley: *Hey, beautiful!*

I instantly get butterflies in my stomach, forgetting the fear I just had or the uncertainty I just felt.

Me: *Hi Bradley. How's your morning?*

Bradley: *It's good, thinking of you.*

Oh my gosh, I'm getting all hot and bothered, and now I can't wait to see him again.

Bradley: *I would like to see you tonight if that's okay?*

Taking the words right out of my mouth.

Me: *I can always come to you, or you and Annabelle*

can come over to my place. It's up to you.

Bradley: *Annabelle and I can come to you. How does seven sound?*

Me: *Perfect, I'm done with my classes for the summer. I will cook.*

Bradley: *I will bring the wine.*

Me: *I guess it's a date.*

Bradley: *Absolutely!*

Swooning and smiling to myself, I drift off into a daydream about last night. I didn't want him to leave, but I knew he had to get home. Shit, what should I make for dinner? I need to go a little early today to prepare. I just might take Dianella up on her offer after all. I want Bradley and Annabelle to feel at home. And really, I just need him to take my mind off of everything.

I head into the kitchen to help with the afternoon rush approaching us sooner than later.

"Dianella, I'm going to take you up on your offer. I have another date with Bradley tonight."

"Ooh, I'm so happy for you, sweetie. Just remember to be careful."

"I will. Thanks, sis. I love you more than you know."

"I love you more." We both giggle and get back to work.

The sun is setting, bringing an incredible skyline to the surface with reds and purples, pinks and orange rays to the atmosphere. I'm in my amazing kitchen making a savory bourbon salmon with wild rice and fresh asparagus paired with a delicate white wine, even though Bradley said he would bring a bottle. I didn't tell him what I was cooking. Oh, well, shrugging my shoulders. He won't mind.

I set the table for two and pull a highchair to the table. I bought three for when the triplets come over, so Lily doesn't always have to tote her entire house with her. I have soft jazz playing on the surround sound when I hear my doorbell.

"Coming." He's right on time. I love punctuality in a man, but I would have let him slide because he has an eight-month-old baby to get ready too. I run and open the door, and I see the most amazingly handsome man standing at my door. He's wearing light blue jeans, cut up, that enhance his tight ass, with a pretty sky-blue V-neck that makes his biceps look three times bigger. He's wearing white Cole Haans on his feet, and he looks sexy as hell. If he didn't have Annabelle in his hands right now, I would jump his bones.

I step aside, letting him walk past me. "Please come in." He glides in like Annabelle weighs nothing to him. He wraps his free hand around my waist and brings his lips down to mine. He's so much taller than I am, so I stand on my tippy toes to reach him. He gives me a delicate kiss on my lips and swipes his tongue over my mouth to gain access. I grant him permission, and oh my god, his lips, his tongue exploring my inner soul is the most erotic thing I've ever experienced with my mouth. He pulls away, and I almost fall forward. He steadies me on my feet and gives me his sexy smirk on his face.

"Hey, beautiful." I'm totally a lost for words, like completely speech-less and almost forget Annabelle is even there until she starts giggling. Then, finally, I gather my wits and close the door.

"Hi," I say more to Annabelle than I say to him. I've already fallen head over heels for this precious girl. He snickers and carry her to the living area. "Please make yourself at home. Dinner is almost ready."

"It smells divine. I can't wait to taste it. Wow, you are definitely prepared."

"What do you mean?" I glance over my shoulder.

"You have a highchair and toys for Annabelle to play with."

"Oh, yes. The triplets come over once a week to give Lily and Jason a break, even though Lily hates the thought of leaving her kids for more than a few hours. It took a lot of convincing from Jason and me to get her on board. But, once she came over and saw how prepared I was, she calmed a little at the idea. So instead of fifty calls and text messages, she has dropped to twenty."

We both burst out laughing. "I know the feeling. You always feel you're the only one who can protect your kids, so I completely understand. It kills me to leave Annabelle all day."

"You know, I can watch her if you like. I have a room set up for my niece and nephews. I can certainly add to it. It will be a little daycare by the time I'm finished with it."

"I'll take you up on your offer someday."

"Great!" I prepare the plates and set them on the dining table. I pour the glasses of wine. "Dinner is served."

He picks Annabelle up out of her car seat and places her in the high-chair. "She's already eaten, so she will be content with her toys."

"Okay, but if she needs anything, I have everything from food to pampers and toys."

"Thank you."

"Anytime, Annabelle is so precious."

I say the blessings, and we start to eat. "Oh, wow. This is really good."

I smile, "What, you didn't know I could cook too?"

"Oh, no, it's not that…."

"It's okay. I'm just messing with you." He takes a noticeable breath and continues eating.

"No, really, this is amazing. It tastes just like a five-star restaurant chef prepared this meal for us."

"Well, thank you."

"Hats off to the chef. Where did you learn to cook like this?"

"My sister. She raised me on her own and always said I needed to learn how to do things on my own because she might not always be around. She was really preparing me for her death, not so much for my future."

"Wow, sorry to hear that."

"No, it's okay. I'm glad she taught me. It gave us a bond I wouldn't trade for the world."

"That's good. My mom taught me how to cook. I'm going to have to show you a little something someday."

"I would love that," tearing us both away, Annabelle starts crying a little while playing with her toys.

"It's her bedtime."

"Okay." We finish our dinner, and I escort him and Annabelle to the nursery.

"Holy shit, you weren't kidding. You have everything in this room."

"Yeah, I probably went overboard, but nothing but the best for my niece and nephews."

"I can see that."

"Here, you can sit in the rocking chair. I will sit on the love seat." He sits down with Annabelle in his arms, and he starts to rock her back and forth. He then starts to sing a lullaby, and I'm astonished by the sound of his voice.

Holy fuck, he can sing.

I don't say a word because I don't want to interrupt. I just sit there mesmerized by his soothing voice. Hell, it's so good; I want to drift off to sleep as well. I had no idea he had a voice like that. He sings a couple of chords before Annabelle drifts off to sleep. He stands up gently, and I do the same. I pull back the blanket in one of the cribs, and he gently lies her down. I pull the cover over her and tuck her in. I grab the baby monitor and turn it on to hear her. We then walk out of the room and head for the living room.

The next thing I know, Bradley grabs my arm and spins me around. He presses me against the wall, and I look into his eyes. Behind those sexy grey eyes, I see pure lust. It's undeniable what he wants to do to me. He lifts me up, and I wrap my legs around his waist. He pushes my arms above my head and pins me to the wall. I still have the monitor in my hand, and I hold on tightly so I don't drop it. He thrusts his tongue into my mouth and devours me like it's his last meal on earth. I close my eyes and get ready for a ride of a lifetime. He tastes of wine and salmon, and he tastes so damn good. He pulls me off the wall and carries me to my bedroom in his strong arms. He hasn't taken his mouth off mine.

We enter my bedroom, and he places me on the bed and climbs on top of me, still kissing me. He then pulls his lips from mine, and I feel lost without them. Finally, he slides one of my straps down from my shoulder and kisses me along my neckline.

"Oh my god, that feels so good." I forget the monitor is in my hand when I hear soft snores from it. I release it from my hand and run my hands over his gentle waves. He continues to kiss me and doesn't say a word. It's almost like he was waiting for this moment all day. I couldn't tell earlier. I guess he acts a certain way around his daughter or of course I'm overthinking things once again.

He then reaches under my dress and lifts it up. Next, he reaches behind my back and unfastens my bra, releasing my breast for his desirable pleasure. My breasts are a little big for my frame, yet perky all the same. Finally, he takes one of my nipples in his mouth, and I nearly fall apart.

"Oh shit, Bradley. I—" He continues to suck and nip at my nipple while playing and pulling at the other. I can feel my arousal soaking my panties, and I don't want him to stop.

He lifts up and takes a deep breath. "Holy shit Amelia, baby, I can smell you." I'm not sure if that's a good thing or a bad thing, but at this point, I'm not embarrassed, nor do I care. Then, he starts to take my panties off and abandon my breast altogether. It's like a kid in a candy store; he has no idea what he wants more or next. But the second he puts my panties to his nose, I fall apart. It's the second most erotic thing I've ever seen.

"Fuck, you smell fucking delicious." He then drops to his knees, fully dressed, and takes my pussy into his mouth. He swipes his tongue over my clit, and just like that, I fall apart all over again. "That's it, baby. Give it to me. Give me all of you." He licks, and he tucks at my clit, and it's the most amazing feeling I've ever felt in my life. This is even better than the first time.

While licking my clit he inserts two fingers inside me, and I feel my hips buck off the bed. "That's it, baby. I want you to come in my mouth." And as if on command, my pussy gives him what he wants, again. And again, I feel the electricity running through my body and into my pussy.

"Shit, Bradley!" He continues with his assault on my pussy and then lifts up and takes off his shirt. And oh my god, he looks like a model in a magazine. His flat stomach and chiseled eight pack are to die for, and those massive arms, oh my gosh. I hit the jackpot with this sexy ass man of gods. He then drops his jeans and boxer, and his dick is standing at least ten inches of solid muscle. Holy fuck. I was scared before, but I'm amazed now. How the hell did that fit inside of me? Next, he tears open a condom and place it on that long, colossal dick. How the hell does the condom even fit on him? He's so big.

He then climbs back on top and looks into my eyes, "Baby, this may hurt a little. I'm sorry."

"Why are you sorry?"

"Because I didn't wait until you healed. I wanted you all fucking day, and I can't wait another minute. I will be as gentle as possible. If it hurts too much, just let me know. I will stop. Okay?"

I nod my head. "Baby, I need to hear you say it."

"Okay," I blurt out. "I'm fine. I will be okay. I can handle pain." He takes a deep breath and pushes through my tight walls, and at first, it hurts a little, but not as bad as the first time. He closes his eyes, feeling and absorbing every part of me. How does he feel anything with a condom on? He continues to push through, and at this point, I feel completely full. I can feel his balls brush up against my ass, and I can feel his dick twitching inside my pussy. Just his touch alone is electrifying. He begins to push in and out, and my toes begin to curl. He reaches under my legs and presses my knees to my chest, and holy fuck, that feels fucking amazing. This angle is so intense, I want more.

"Please, Bradley."

"What do you want, baby?" grunting through his teeth. He makes me tell him what I want, and I get all hot and bothered all over again.

"I want you to go deeper, faster. Please?" I pant.

He then picks up the speed and gives me exactly what I want.

"Fuck, baby, you feel fucking great," he says through clenched teeth. I then feel that same feeling rush over me and think I'm about to come.

"Bradley, I think I'm about to come."

"Yes, baby. Come all over this dick." He continues to thrust inside of me and do this twirling thing with his hips causing his dick to swirl inside of me and holy fuck, that feels fucking amazing.

"Shit Bradley. Fuck." I arch my back off the bed and feel my insides explode. I feel my pussy tighten more, and I can't feel my toes.

"Fuck Amelia. You about to make me come after that performance." He continues to thrust through my orgasm, giving me an even more intense pleasure. I feel his dick swelling inside me and don't know how he can get any bigger. "Fuck baby, I'm coming!" His eyes roll in the back of his head, and I feel the condom fill up with his seed.

He falls down on top of me, letting my legs go but catches himself with his forearms, so he won't crush me. He kisses me on the forehead and rolls off of me. He heads into the bathroom to clean himself off.

Once he returns to the bedroom, he gets in next to me and pulls me to his chest. "Baby, that was amazing. That thing you do with your pussy, drives me insane."

"What do you mean?"

"You clinch down on my dick, and when you do that, it gives even more pleasure."

"Oh, I had no idea."

"You keep doing that, and I'm never gonna wanna leave."

We both giggle, and he pulls me tighter in his arms and kisses me on my forehead.

"How do you feel anything with a condom on?"

"Well, it's the friction I feel more than anything. It's nothing like going bare, but I believe in protecting us both."

"Oh no, I wasn't questioning why you wear it; I just wonder how you feel anything. That's all."

"I understood the question; I just like to be open with you about everything."

"Thank you for that."

"As long as we are honest to each other, nothing can come between us." I feel him physically tense, however it disappears just as quickly as it appeared.

"I'm glad you wear a condom. I'm not on the pill yet, so I will rather be safe than sorry."

"When will you be?"

"I have an appointment on Monday with my gynecologist. She will explain to me what's best for me. I never really needed to be because my cycles are regular, and I was never sexually active. However, both my sisters insisted that I go."

"They're right, you know. If Tyra and I were safe, Annabelle wouldn't be here, but then again, she wouldn't be here, and I can't imagine life without her. I love her so much."

"Yes, I see how much you both love each other. You're doing an amazing job with her. She's such a precious girl."

"Thank you. It really wasn't a choice in the matter for me. I knew what I had to do, and I did it."

"I admire you for that. And I meant what I said, I'm always here to help."

"Thank you." He tucks his face into my neck and kisses me gently. I feel his dick awaken, and I know he must want more.

"If you want to make love again, I'm okay. It didn't hurt as much as the first time."

"It's okay, baby. I can wait until the morning. I just want to hold you in my arms right now."

"Okay." After a few minutes, we both relax and drift off to sleep in each other arms.

∾

I wake up in the morning with Bradley between my legs, licking my pussy. It feels so fucking good; I don't bother telling him to stop.

Why would I?

"Oh my god." I moan. He continues to nip on my pussy, and I feel myself coming all over again. Holy shit, how many times can I come within a twenty-four-hour period?

"That's it, baby, come in my mouth." I arch my back off the bed and explode in his mouth. He laps every bit of my essence. He places another condom on, gets on top of me, and thrusts his dick inside of me, filling me up completely. It takes me a second to adjust to the intrusion, but once I'm wide awake, he fucks me fast and hard. This is entirely different from the first two times. This is more of a need, so I let him take from me as much as he wants and desires.

"Bradley, I'm yours. Take what you need from me."

And just like that, he slams me deeper into the mattress. I hold on tight for the ride and I'm ready to come with every thrust. I feel myself building and prepared to come once again.

"Fuck Amelia, I'm about to come."

"So am I," I pant between breaths.

We then both come together, and it's the most blissful moment we've ever had together. I feel him throbbing inside of me while I clench him tighter with my walls. Then, finally, we both sigh and collapse on the bed.

"That was the best wake-up call in the world. I don't mind doing that again."

"That was fucking amazing. I can't get enough of you." He rolls off of me and goes into the bathroom to clean up.

"There are towels and washcloths in the bottom draw and extra toothbrushes."

"Why do you have extra toothbrushes?"

"Well, when my sisters or friends get drunk downtown, they crash in my third bedroom. So they usually need a toothbrush and other things when they come over their hangover."

"You're amazing, you know that?"

"I try." I hear him turn on the shower, and I sit up in the bed. I then hear little giggles on the baby monitor, and that's my cue to go get Annabelle cleaned up.

I leave Bradley in the bathroom, grab my robe, and head to the nursery. Annabelle is reaching up at the different animals on the mobile over her. I look into the crib, and she lights up when she sees me. I reach down and pick her up to change her and get her ready for the day.

"Oh, my goodness. You're so cute, my precious. Yes, you are, yes, you are."

I then take her into the kitchen to give her a bath in the sink.

I place her on the counter on a blanket and then remove her clothes, and her pamper. I pick her up and set her on my hip while running her warm water. Next, I grab the baby wash and shampoo. I then clean her in the sink, and she splashes her hands in the water.

"Ah, you like playing in the water."

"Yes, she loves bath time." I look up, startled, and Bradley is standing at the island, watching me clean Annabelle. He's wearing a pair of washed-out jeans with a white t-shirt. "You look like a natural."

"I think it's the nurture in me. I love children and would love to have some one day."

"Really?"

"Absolutely! I want at least two or three or more. I'm not really picky. Children bring joy to your life, and watching them transform before your eyes, is an amazing opportunity. I want to experience that too."

I finish washing Annabelle's hair and rinse her off. I then wrap a towel around her and bring her to my chest.

"I have a change of clothes for her in the bag." Bradley heads to the living area and grabs the baby bag. I look around and realize the dining table and the kitchen is clean.

"Hey, did you clean up?"

"Yeah, it's the least I can do for that delicious meal and dessert last night."

I blush a little, "Thank you, but I could have taken care of it."

"And have you make the food and clean up? I think not. Especially when I'm around."

He hands me the clothes, and I get Annabelle dressed, and I do her hair. Her hair is so long and curly; therefore, I put it up in two ponytails. "Now, let me look at you. You look so pretty in your yellow dress and pigtails." Bradley goes into the kitchen and makes coffee, and then starts breakfast. I can get used to this.

"How do you want your coffee?"

"With a little creamer, and that's it."

"Okay, coming right up."

I place Annabelle in the highchair, and I grab bananas and baby cereal from the pantry. I mix it up and start feeding her while Bradley cooks breakfast.

Annabelle is so good with me, and it makes me fall in love with her even more. I hear a phone ping and think it's mine, so I grab it.

Tyra: *Where the fuck are you?*

I stare at the text, totally shocked at what I see. After a moment of gathering my thoughts, finally, I turn the phone over and realize it's not my phone; it's Bradley's.

"Uh, Bradley. I think the phone is for you."

He turns around and sees my expression and his demeanor automatically changes. He wipes his hands on a kitchen towel, reaches for the phone, and looks at it.

"Shit. I'm sorry you had to see that."

"Who is it?"

"It's Tyra. Ever since they let her out of the hospital, she's called me and texted me. I've been meaning to get my number changed; I've just haven't had the time."

"What does she want?" I ask with concern in my voice.

"She wants Annabelle and me back. She doesn't understand why I left."

"Are you concerned that she would try to take Annabelle from you?"

"No, not at all. She has no idea where we are, and I plan to keep it that way. She will not be any harm to you or Annabelle," he assures me after probably seeing the concern in my face. "Now, breakfast is served," changing the subject.

CHAPTER 7

TYRA

Finally, I'm out of that hellhole. I give it to those guys; they did what they promised. Now, I need to keep my end of the deal.

I need to find Bradley. And I need to find him now.

He refuses to respond to any of my calls or texts. So, where to start.

"Ah, ha."

Let's start with his pride and joy.

"*His dearest mommy.*"

CHAPTER 8

BRADLEY

Sitting in my office looking over my files, my mind drifts back to the conversation Amelia and I had this morning. I felt the vibe change after talking about Tyra. I know she's worried and has every right to be. But, if I want to start something with Amelia and make it last, I need to cut Tyra out of my life.

But how do you do that to the mother of your child?

How can you just stop a mother from being in their child's life?

Even though I don't love her anymore, I still have love for her because she's my child's mother. I can't treat her like that.

"Ugh, this is so fucked up," I blurt out.

"What's fucked up?" Claire asks when she walks into my office. Throwing me off completely, I look up.

"Nothing. You have something for me?" I ask, not feeling particularly kind today. She really should have knocked before she entered.

"Uh, yes. Mrs. Megan asked me to give you these accounts and to tell you, you have a visitor." She puts the files on my desk and stands there waiting for something.

"Um, you can send them back."

"Oh, yes. Of course sir," she answers nervously, turns around, and walks out.

I know she was the best candidate, but she has a week to get it together, or I will have to let her go. I need someone like Mrs. Megan. Now, that lady knows what she's doing.

"Hey Bradley, I thought you would like to go out for lunch this afternoon," says Amelia when she walks in. My entire mood changes when I see her angelic face. God, this girl means more to me in the few months we've known each other than Tyra has ever meant to me. I love it when she wears her hair curly like that and a short navy blue sundress showing off her incredible legs.

Claire stands at the door, watching our exchange, and has a look of disappointment on her face. "Uh, Claire?"

"Yes, sir," tearing her gaze from Amelia.

"That's all I need. Can you close the door on your way out?"

"Sure thing." She then walks out with apparent rage in her eyes.

Once she closes the door, I drift my focus back to the beautiful angel before me. "What a pleasant surprise. I needed a break, so you're definitely right on time."

"Perfect, because I'm about to take you to Flock to the Wok."

"Flock to the what?" I ask, confused but mesmerized by her beauty. I pull her into my arms while I lean against the desk. Her sundress shifts as she approaches, and I just want to snatch it off her instead, but I'll be a gentleman.

"It's Asian cuisine, and it's delicious. I'm good friends with the owners."

"Wherever you go, I will follow."

"I bet you will." She flashes me a cute little devilish smirk with attitude, but it looks sexy on her no matter how much attitude she tries to display. She pushes out of my embrace and walks towards the door swaying her hips with every step. Fuck, she's sexy as hell. I gather my wits and follow her out the door.

We run into Ryan on the way out.

"Hi Ryan, it's been so long." Amelia wraps her arms around his neck, giving him the biggest hug and a kiss on the cheek. If I didn't know them so well, I would have been boiling with jealous rage about their interaction.

"Hey, baby girl. I know, I've been busy with Kimberly and the baby. Our boy has been kicking her ass."

"I bet." He glances my way and spreads a smile across his face.

"So, where are y'all off to?"

"Headed out for lunch, something about flocking to the wok," I say, and at my expense, everyone laughs at me. "What?"

Amelia wraps her arms around my waist. "Babe, you will love it."

"Okay, you two. Have fun. Oh, and Amelia, Kimberly told me what happened the other night. I'm glad you're okay and know we're here if you need us."

"I know." And we walkout. "We're taking my car. No arguments." I put my hands up, surrendering to her demands. "No complaints from me."

"Good."

We walk up to her car, and it's no other than a Mercedes S500 black in color. It's one of my dream cars.

"Holy shit, you have a Mercedes S500?"

"Yes, I drove my sister's a couple of times and fell in love with it. It was either this or the G-Class Wagon."

I look at her in astonishment. "How do you afford something like this?" Fuck, just realizing just how completely disrespectful that statement is, "Shit, I did mean it that way," I spill apologetically.

"No, its okay. No need to apologize. Remember I told you my parents died?"

"Yeah."

"Well, they left my sister and me a large sum of money and assets. So we actually want for nothing, I just prefer to work while I'm in school, and once I get my nursing licenses, I plan on working at the hospital."

"I knew Ryan and Jason were loaded, but I had no idea you were too."

"Yeah, I just don't act like it. But, hell, none of us do."

"I see. I've been saving every penny I can to get back on my feet. Ryan has offered to help, but I refused. I believe in getting my own."

"I understand that." We get into her car and head to the restaurant everyone is raving about. We pull into her garage and park.

"We're heading to your house?"

"No, babe. It's free parking, well technically, I pay for the parking, so truthfully, it's not free, but at least we don't have to search for any. The restaurant is a block over."

"Okay, understandable." We get out of the car and head to the restaurant. Once we get there, it's completely packed with people. "Are you sure you want to eat here? We can always go somewhere else."

"Here let me speak with the hostess." Amelia walks over and speak to the hostess. I take my phone out to check some emails when I see two guys on the corner. They appear to be watching us, but I brush it off. I have to get out the idea of cop life and understand that not all people are out to harm me or someone. Besides, it's been a while since I left the department. If someone was looking for me, they would have already.

Amelia comes back, "They have a waiting list for an hour. What if we head to the JW Marriott on River Street? They have different options there."

"Cool, lead the way." I put my phone in my back pocket and snake my fingers into Amelia's. Her hands are so soft and inviting. Amelia guides us down Whitaker Street towards the river. We decide to cut through Williamson Street and approach these stairs that looks like they will kill you if you even blink a little. And of course there's a sign that says 'Use at your own Risk.' "Are you sure you want to take those stairs," I ask with concern in my tone.

"Oh, please, I use these stairs all the time. There's nothing to be afraid of. They're only called the Stair of Death. You only die, if you're not careful," she waves off nonchalantly.

"Right," glancing down below, I hastily, but cautiously step down, but before my foot touches the first step, two dudes approach us, blocking our path to the restaurant. We try to maneuver around them, when they block us again. I recognize the guys from the corner at Flock to the Wok restaurant. I slightly push Amelia behind me. "Can we help you?"

"Naw, my nigga, we want the girl."

"You ain't getting the girl, my nigga, so back the fuck off," my senses on high alert now. Should have paid attention to my intuition before. Amelia pulls on my arm, urging me to leave it alone.

"We ain't leaving until she comes with us." They both pull out a gun, and I jump into survival mode. I have to protect her at all costs. Without another thought, I pull out my weapon I keep tucked in my back jeans. I have two targets, and I must eliminate both. They're so concerned with her; they don't realize I'm armed. I point and pull the trigger at one of the guys, shooting him in the head. I push Amelia out of the way while I pull the trigger and hit the other guy in the throat, not allowing any of them to get off a shot.

Shit!!!

Amelia is on the phone dialing 9-1-1 when I turn to see if there's any other threat. I run to her side once the coast is clear.

"Baby, are you okay?" Tears are running down her face, and she's totally terrified, beyond freaked the fuck out. I pull her into my arms and grab the phone out of her trembling fingers.

"Hello?"

"Yes, this is 911, is everyone okay?"

"My girl and I are okay. I shot and killed two suspects who were trying to kidnap my girlfriend. We're on the top of the Stairs of Death on Williamson Street, just above River Street.

"And your name, sir?"

"Detective Bradley Philips from Jacksonville Police Department."

Amelia pulls out of my arms when she hears my confession. "You're a cop?" she questions with confusion.

"Yes, babe. I'm a cop. I've been in hiding for two years. I was in the process of retiring when Ryan approached me with an opportunity."

"Does he know, you're — "

"Yes, he does. I just couldn't tell anyone because I've been under-cover for four years, and I couldn't blow my cover."

"Sir, are you still there?" I hear the operator ask.

"I don't understand. Why wouldn't you tell me? pausing, she shakes her head back and forth. "So, everything has been a lie?" backing away from me like she's afraid of me; like she doesn't trust me.

"No, baby. I have not lied to you; I just kept this from you because I needed to protect you and Annabelle," reaching for her, she pulls away from me abruptly.

She begins to shake her head and drop down to her knees. "I'm such an idiot. I really thought we had something, but you've been lying to me this whole time," screaming at me even louder.

I reach for her again, and she pushes me off of her. "No, don't touch me. I can't deal with this right now."

"Sir, are you still there?" I hear the operator ask again and of course I ignore her, again.

"Baby, please. I never meant to hurt you. I care about you." I hear the sirens, and she stumbles to her feet. I give her space because I don't want to push her.

Jason runs up to her and brings her into an embrace. That should be me, not him, fuck. "Amelia, sweetie, are you okay?"

"Yes, I'm fine. Those guys are the guys you're looking for. Apparently, they did recognize me," she spits out sarcastically. "They were trying to take me when Bradley shot and killed both of them," pausing for what seemed forever. "He saved me." Hearing herself confess those words, she looks up at me, and at that moment, I'm fucking terrified. I have no idea what she's thinking. "Bradley saved me." She walks up to me and grabs me by the jacket. She plants one hell of a kiss on my lips, and I physically melt in her arms. Fuck, I thought I lost her forever, warping my arms around her small waist. She pulls away, and I feel lost without her lips on mine.

"Thank you, Bradley."

"Baby, I love you. I will do anything to protect you. I promise you that."

She looks into my eyes as if she's searching for something. "I'm still furious that you lied to me or whatever, but I can't think about that right now." I pull her closer to me, forgetting that there are two dead bodies next to us, reporters all over the place and standing in an active crime scene. Not caring that she didn't return the same feeling for me, my life belongs to her and Annabelle.

～

We never made it to lunch, so once the crime scene was cleaned up, we headed to my house to pick up Annabelle and grab a few items. Amelia wanted us to stay with her for the weekend, and I don't blame her. She has really been through a lot.

After reviewing the cameras and comparing the sketch composite, it turns out that those guys that were after Amelia were soldiers. They were being robbed by the two guys they shot but got scared and ran. When they saw Amelia on the news the next day as a possible witness, they wanted to shut her up. Little did they know she was dating a cop and a sharpshooter. So, they got a little more than they bargained for. If they had just turned themselves in, they would have been fine, and the guy who survived the shooting would have been charged with robbery and aggravated assault.

Amelia doesn't say anything on the ride to my house. She just looks out the window watching the scenery. But, once we pull up, she lifts her head up.

"I know this place. It belongs to Ryan. I was going to buy it from him, but I decided to live further downtown."

"Yeah, he's letting me rent it until I can find my own place."

"That was nice of him."

"Yeah, he's a pretty stand-up guy."

"That he is."

We get out of the car and head into the house.

"You did a wonderful job with the décor. I love it," she says matter-of-factly, almost like she trying hard to make small talk.

"Thanks."

I head into the living area and find Daphne and Annabelle taking a nap. I gently shake Daphne, and she startles awake.

"Hey, Daphne."

"Hi, Mr. Bradley. Sorry, we just dozed off for a little nap. Is everything okay?"

"Oh yes, I got off work early and decided to pick up Annabelle and give you the rest of the weekend off."

"Oh, okay. She just finished eating, and I already changed her. We also went to the park for about an hour." She gets up and grabs her things. "If you need anything, please let me know. I'm available all weekend."

"Okay, thank you, Daphne, and wait, here's your payment for the week," pulling cash out of my wallet.

"Oh, thank you, Mr. Bradley. Have a good weekend." She turns around and sees Amelia standing near the kitchen.

"Oh, I'm sorry. I didn't see you there. Hi, how are you?" She extends her hand to shake Amelia's. Amelia grabs it.

"No, it's okay. I didn't want to interrupt. My name is Amelia. It's nice to meet you."

"I'm Daphne. Oh, wait. You work at the cafe down the street, right?" Daphne asks Amelia.

"Yes, I help manage it."

"Right, I go there all the time." Her smile brighting her features. "Hope to see you again." She smiles and then prepares to walk out but turns back around. "Oh, I almost forgot. Mr. Bradley, a woman, was watching Annabelle at the park today. At first, I didn't think anything of it, but then some of the other babysitters felt a little weird about it, so I sent you a text because I knew you were working."

Raising my concern, "Do you remember what she looked like?"

"Yes. A dark-skinned Black woman about your age with a wig on. She didn't approach us or anything; she was just watching us. Then, shortly after, I brought Annabelle home. It just gave me a weird vibe, and I wanted to let you know."

"Thanks, Daphne. I appreciate it." She then walks out.

"Fuck!" Amelia comes to my side.

"It's your ex, isn't it? Tyra, Annabelle's mom?"

"Yes. She found us. Fuck, how the fuck did she find us?"

"Baby, we can't stay here. Tyra knows where you are, and she probably forced it out of someone close to you. We have to go. I know this is not what you expected, but you can do this. If not for me, then for Annabelle."

I then look over at Annabelle and snap out of my trans. I can't let that crazy bitch hurt my daughter. I stand up and head for the room, taking three steps at a time. I grab my suitcase and Annabelle's suitcase. I fill it up with all kinds of shit. I then head to Annabelle's room and grab all her shit too. I'm moving at rapid speed because I can't let anything happen to her.

I have to protect her.

I hurry to the living room with the luggage in my hands. Amelia already has Annabelle in her car seat and ready to go. I guide her to the door and head towards the car. Amelia places Annabelle in the backseat and gets in with her. I get in the driver's seat and drive off, headed towards Amelia's home.

I hear Amelia playing with Annabelle in the backseat and giggling and cooing. Probably trying to keep her mind off the shit storm we continue to enter. Annabelle really likes Amelia. Man, am I glad for that. But, I need to protect both of them at all costs. I have no idea what Tyra is up to.

I drive around the block to ensure we're not being followed by Tyra. I then pull up in the garage. Amelia grabs Annabelle, and I grab the suitcases from the trunk. We take the elevator to her home, enter the door, and she locks it behind us. I then canvas the entire house to ensure all windows are closed and locked. Finally, I return to the living area and find Amelia and Annabelle playing on the floor.

"You have to calm down. Kids can sense fear, sadness, and anger. If you need a break, go out on the patio. I will bring you a drink in a few."

I head to the balcony and take a seat, realizing she's so right. This crazy bitch got me right where she wants me, I'm panicking like a little bitch, and now Amelia is pissed at me. What the fuck am I going to do?

CHAPTER 9

AMELIA

I wanted Bradley and Annabelle to stay with me because, for whatever reason, I got a bad feeling about everything. I know those assholes can't hurt me, but I still have this feeling of uneasiness, almost like someone watching me or something. And now that we know Tyra is in town for sure, I thought it would be best for all three of us to stay together.

My loft has four bedrooms, a master bedroom, a room I converted into a dance studio, the nursery for the triplets, and a guest bedroom. I let Annabelle stay in the nursery since it's already equipped with everything she will need.

"I can take the guest bedroom. I don't mind at all," Bradley offers. I should make him suffer a little after what he pulled.

"Sure, that's a good idea. Thanks for suggesting it. I'll bring you some towels and washcloths," looking devastated and tormented, he stretches his hand out.

"Lead the way." I walk past him down the hall. I first stop at the linen closet and grab a few more towels, hand towels, and washcloths. I then continue down the hall past the dance studio and enter the third bedroom.

"The room has its own bathroom. Here are a few extra towels." I hand the bundle over to Bradley, and he reluctantly takes it. He places the towels and his bag on the bed, and he pulls me into his arms.

I feel the undeniable electricity run through my veins and into the womb of my stomach instantly. I love him too; I just don't know if I can trust him right now. "Baby, I know it will take time for you to trust me again, but I promise you I will do everything in my power to get you back."

I look into his eyes, and I push away, gently feeling the connection tear between us. "Please don't make promises you can't keep."

"I never do." And at that moment, I see the sincerity in his eyes and know he means what he says, but I still need time to think. I need time to process this before I lose my shit, completely.

"If you need anything else, I'll be in the kitchen cooking. Is there anything particular you would like for dinner tonight?"

"Whatever you make, I'm sure it will be just fine. Oh, and Amelia?"

"Yes," pausing at the door.

"Thank you."

"For what?" turning around to search his face.

"For letting Annabelle and I stay here."

"Bradley, you're doing me the favor, remember?"

"Nonetheless, thank you. It means more to me than you know."

"You're welcome." I then walk out of the room and rush to my room, close the door and break down like I never broke down before.

My heart aching, and my mind spinning. I feel like I felt all those years ago when my parents died. For years I wondered why me and not them? Why did I survive and not them? Lily needed them; I needed them.

I need him.

I lay on the floor and find myself crying and crying until I can't cry anymore, and then find a way to cry some more. What is going on with you, Amelia? My anxiety on overload.

Well, for starters, you witnessed a shooting, tried to save a person's life who probably didn't deserve it, and then those very people tried to come after you and hurt you.

They tried to scare you. They tried to break you.

But I've become an expert at locking away my feelings. It's so easy to hide my pain behind a mask...a smile. Sad how so few care to look deeper.

But your knight in shining armor didn't falter. He didn't let anything happen. At that moment, he was someone totally different. He was my shield, my protector in that moment I needed him the most. So, why am I so tortured right now?

Amelia, he lied to you.

He kept something essential from you, and that's why you're upset. That's why you're hurting. Even though he said he was protecting you, it's the principle. If he really loved me, he should have told me.

I feel hands lift me up, and I literally jump out of my skin. Just that quick, I forgot Bradley was even here in the other room.

"Baby, it's me. I heard you crying, and I don't think you should be alone."

"Just leave me alone," I choke out between snotty sobs.

"I'm not leaving you, not like this."

Knowing exactly what I needed to hear, I let him pick me up, put me in his lap while he rocks me back and forth, and I just cry and cry some more. The fire within is replaced by fear as the anxiety eats me alive. The darkness crept in until the light inside eventually died. Finally, he wraps his strong arms around me and blankets me with his strength. I felt completely out of control until he came to my rescue yet again.

"It's okay. I'm not going to leave you. I'm right here," pressing my head to his chest, he starts humming to himself while soothing me with his embrace. I never knew how soothing this could be. His very touch has calmed me completely, and I start to feel better. His voice is hypnotizing, and I wonder why he doesn't sing more. I find myself taking slow deep breaths, and, in that moment, I feel safer than I ever felt before.

"Amelia, do you feel better? Are you able to stand?"

"I'm fine. Thank you. I'm so sorry. I didn't mean for you to hear all of that."

"Amelia, look at me." I lift my gaze and look into his eyes. My god, his eyes are mesmerizing, yet full of fear. "It's okay to break down. It's okay to be upset. It's okay to be afraid and lose control. But, it's not okay to keep it bottled up. You're a strong woman, but even strong women need a little help sometimes. That's why I'm here. Lean on me. Let me be your strength. I'm sorry for not being completely honest with you. I should have told you about my past. I know that now, and I will not keep anything else from you. You have my word."

"I just don't understand why you kept it from me. I find that being more prepared is better than being half-cocked and unprepared. What if something happened and I had no clue what was going on. It could have been awful. You get that, right?" I quiz.

"Yes, of course, I get that. I just thought I was protecting you by not telling you."

"What's so bad that you couldn't be honest with me?"

He takes a deep breath before he answers the question. "Well, I was drafted right out of the academy, so not even the officers knew that I was a cop undercover. I dealt with some pretty bad people who were involved in drugs and sex trafficking."

"Sex trafficking? Kim was sold by her parents into sex trafficking."

"Yes, I know. I found out later after bringing down the operation. I also found officers, lawyers, doctors, and government officials involved. I was in so deep I started to forget who I was as a person. I watched innocent girls get raped and beaten, and I couldn't take it anymore. I even did some evil shit that I'm not proud of. It makes me sick to my stomach just thinking about it. So, once we could get enough evidence to put those assholes away, I asked to get out. I didn't want anything to do with that life anymore, and I couldn't trust the officers I was working with on the streets anymore, so I left. Everyone assumed I was injured and retired, but in actuality, I left because I didn't have the stomach for it anymore. And some people want me dead for messing with their livelihood. Tyra had just gotten pregnant and had problems, but I wasn't always there because of the job and my own mental state. So, when she started to have mood swings, I just thought it was the pregnancy, and it would pass. But I later found out that she's bipolar and has signs of schizophrenia. It's my fault that she's the way she is. I was never there to protect her or help her because I was too involved in work. I was too fucked up in my own shit."

"Babe, that's not your fault. How were you supposed to know she was suffering?"

"I should have been there. Maybe what she did to Annabelle would have never happened if I saw the signs."

"Even if you saw the signs, you wouldn't have been able to help. Tyra has to want to help herself. She has to want to take the treatments. No one can force her to do it, not even a judge. That's the disease of mental health illness. This is not your fault, and besides, if this had never happened, you would have never met me. I believe things happen for a reason, whether it's good or bad."

"I guess you're right. I just hate that it had to happen like this."

"I get it. I do have another question," not really wanting to ask, but I'm going to ask anyway. I need to know.

"What's that?"

"What horrific thing did you do while undercover?"

"Please don't make me say it," he begs.

"I need to know."

Pausing for what seemed like a lifetime, "I raped a woman too. They made me do it to prove I wasn't a cop. That's why I deserve everything that happens to me. I fucking hate myself for what I've done." I then wrap my arms around his waist, and we just sit on the floor in each other's embrace.

How on earth do I forgive this man for this...*how?*

God, if you hear my prayer... please help us get through this.

I hear a loud bang, and it wakes me up. I look around my bedroom. I then pick up my phone, and it's two in the morning. I then hear another bang and realize it's coming from outside. I get up and go look out the window, but I don't see anything. I hear the noise again, and I think it's coming from the garage this time. I slip on my shoes and head for the elevator. The noise gets louder. So, I take my phone out of my pocket when the doors open. I then see a Black woman throwing a large rock through the window of my car and start running from the garage.

"Oh my gosh. What the hell?" I look at my car, and it's completely destroyed with busted windows and dents all over. I run back to the elevator and take it back to the loft. Once the doors open up, I yell for Bradley to get up.

"Bradley, someone just busted out the windows of my car!"

Entirely startled by my yelling, "Did you call 9-1-1?" he asks while he puts his shoes on.

"No, not yet."

"Call them, and I'll head down to the garage. Did you see who it was?"

"I think it was a Black woman with a long ponytail. She was wearing a thin, dark-colored jacket. I didn't get a good look at her face. She ran before I could."

"Okay. Stay here. Check on Annabelle for me."

"Shit, Annabelle. I forgot." He heads out the door while I enter Annabelle's room. She's soundly asleep, so I head to my room to get the monitor and call 9-1-1."

"9-1-1 Operator, what is your emergency?"

"Someone just busted out the windows of my car, and once she saw me, she took off running."

"Did you get a good look at the woman?"

"No, not really; her back was towards me when I saw her throw the large rock through the windshield."

"Okay, the police are on their way."

"Okay." I then hang up the phone and head back down to the garage. I decided to take the stairs this time.

"Bradley?"

"Yeah, babe. I'm over here." I head towards him near the car. "I think Tyra did this. I saw the vehicle when it passed, and it looks just like hers."

"Are you sure?"

"Positive."

"Okay, the police are on their way."

They arrived about ten minutes later and took our statements and accessed the damage to my car.

"Are you two going to be okay tonight?" the officer asks.

"Yes, we'll be fine," Bradley answers, obviously frustrated with the whole situation. But, unfortunately, we can't catch a break.

"Okay, well, we will place your home on extra patrol for now. If you need anything, give us a call. In the meantime, try to get some sleep."

"Thank you, officer," I say as they leave the garage.

I grab Bradley's hand. "I'll take care of the damages in the morning; let's go upstairs."

"I will take care of the damages. It's my fault this is even happening to you."

"I have insurance. It will take care of the damage."

"Then I will pay the deductible. You will not suffer because of my past." I know he's serious, so I just drop it and lead him to the elevator. "I'm sorry, Amelia. I never meant to cause you harm or pain."

"Look at me," he ignores me and continues to stare straight ahead. "Look at me," I say more firmly.

He then shifts his gaze towards me. "This isn't your fault. No one could have predicted that she would find where I live and bust my windows out. Besides, it's just a car. We're okay, and Annabelle is okay."

"You're right. I just hate that this will not end. She's playing games, and this needs to stop."

"It will; it just takes time."

CHAPTER 10

TYRA

I see my baby girl for the first time in months. But there's something wrong with her. Why is she smiling like that?

She's at the park with some kid pushing her on the swings. She's laughing and giggling the higher she goes.

Annabelle never laughed.

She never giggled.

"*She never laughed because she never liked you,*" the voice taunts.

She always cried.

"*Because she hates you…*" the voice continues.

"Shut up! She never was this happy with me. The fucking devil is still in her. He must get the hell out of her."

I start noticing other people staring at me.

Fuck them!

The kid grabs Annabelle out of the swing and heads across the street. I stay put for a bit longer. She enters a home and closes the door.

"Well, well, well. Bradley, such an improvement from the shithole we lived in."

The son-of-a-bitch finally shows the hell up. But lookit here, I knew that nigga was fucking someone else.

"She's a pretty little thing," the voice swoons. *"Looks like you've been replaced, and when I say replaced, I mean, damn."*

"Shut the hell up. That bitch ain't got nothing on me. I'll be damned if my Annabelle gonna be calling that bitch mommy. Fuck that shit."

"So, whatcha gonna do about it?" the voice asks.

" Just fucking wait. Just wait and see," seating through clench teeth. "Just fucking wait and see…"

Jacksonville Mayo Clinic is the place to be if you want the best care, so I've been told. Mrs. Philips sure is getting the best care in the tri-area.

I enter the elite hospital and approach the counter. "Hi, can I help you?" the heavy-set White woman standing behind the counter.

"Yes, I'm hear to see my mother, Mrs. Dorothy Philips."

"Hold on just a moment. Do you have your ID?"

"Well, I don't have my ID with me. Can you possibly allow this one time? I've really missed her and really want to see her."

The puts a finger up, like I'm some child. This bitch got the right one.

"Ma'am, it says here, Ms. Dorothy only has one child and it's a male, not a female. He has given instructions not to allow any visitors other than himself. And besides, without ID, you're not crossing this threshold."

"What the fuck you mean I can't see her? She's my fucking mother."

"Ma'am, you don't have to curse at me. I'm simply explaining—"

"Fuck your rules. Either you let me the fuck in or I'll snatch yo wig off, bitch!"

"Security, please escort this woman off the premises. She is no longer welcome."

"Ma'am, please come with us," the security guard demands.

"Fuck you."

He places his hands on my shoulder and start pushing me towards the door.

"This is bullshit. You can't keep me from her!"

The security then pushes me out the door and slams it behind him.

"Fucking prick!"

There has to be another way into that fucking room. There has to be!

Well, Tyra, there's always an employee entrance... you ever thought about that? the voice suggests.

"You right. I'll wait for the perfect moment to enter and she will be mine."

CHAPTER 11

BRADLEY

*I*t's been a month since Amelia's car was damaged. She had to get a new car because the damage was so severe that the insurance company didn't feel it would be worth fixing.

So, she decided to get a 2022 Volvo XC90 SUV black in color with peanut butter interior. It definitely looks sharp, but I still love that S500. I will be getting another car like that very soon.

We haven't seen or heard from Tyra since that night. I guess she got the point to leave us alone, but I'm not so sure about that. She has something up her sleeve; I just have to find out what that might be.

I'm sitting on the balcony with Amelia and Annabelle playing on the wooden planks with toys. I love how Annabelle has really adjusted to everything. She's come to really like Amelia, and Amelia certainly adores her. It seems like Amelia has forgiven me for everything because that night, a month ago, she let me sleep with her in her room. Not that she had a choice in the matter. I kind of told her that a man should protect his woman at all costs. I can't do that in another room down the hall. After that, her walls came crashing down, and we are closer than we ever were before even though she hasn't said the three words I crave the most from her. But I simply will not push her. I know it's going to take some time.

My phone rings and I answer it. "Mr. Philips?"

"Yes."

"I'm sorry to inform you, your mother passed away a couple of hours ago."

The phone slips from my fingers, crashing to the floor. The sound deafening, piercing through the thickening air.

"Bradley, what is it?" Amelia asks in the distance. "Bradley?"

Amelia bends down to get it. My vision blurs, and I can't see straight. My hearing must be going because all I hear is echoing sounds in the distance.

"Hello, sorry about that. Bradley dropped the phone. I'm his girl-friend." A brief pause, and Amelia put the phone on speaker.

"He can hear you."

"Yes, I was saying a woman came to the hospital stating that she was her daughter and would like to visit. I explained to the woman that she only has one child, and he instructed us to not allow any visitors. She became distraught, so we called security. She was then escorted out. This was earlier this morning. One of the nurses saw the same woman leaving your mother's room an hour later. The nurse entered the room and found your mother unresponsive. We're terribly sorry for your loss, and we are doing everything in our power to get to the bottom of this. We will need you to come to the hospital to fill out some forms."

"Okay," Amelia answers for me. She then hangs up the phone.

She drops to her knees and forces me to look at her. "Babe, I need you to take a deep breath. Kids can sense when something is wrong, remember? You do not want to upset Annabelle right now. I will make you a drink and give you a minute.

She gets Annabelle and takes her inside to make me a drink. I take a much needed deep breath, trying to take her advice; she's right. I need to calm the fuck down. I sit back on the lounge chair and find myself thinking of my life, tears flowing down my cheeks uncontrollably. I can't stop them. Everything in me comes spilling out. My chest tightens from the very constriction of air I breathe with every breath. How did I get here? How did I let this happen to my mother, my ex, Annabelle, and Amelia? All this pain occurred because of me. Why? Why me? Why us?

Tyra begged me to quit the force, but I was too involved in my case. I wouldn't listen to her. I thought she was being paranoid, and, in a way, she was, but I still should have done everything I possibly could for her. I should have caught her symptoms a lot sooner. I was working so much to provide for our family I wasn't always there to help her. It took my mother to get sick for me to slow the fuck down, and that's when I started seeing the signs, noticed the anger and confusion in Tyra's behavior.

She was my first love, my first everything. We taught each other how to make love and understand each other's wants and needs. She's why I know how to please Amelia, treat her, and understand her wants and needs. Tyra taught me a lot over the years, I just pushed her to the side, and now she has taken so much from me.

I know in my heart, Tyra did this. Tyra killed my mother.

My mother means the world to me; even though our time was coming to an end, I wasn't expecting it to end like this. I wanted to visit her one more time, tell her how Annabelle was doing, and tell her all about Amelia. She would have loved Amelia. I know she would have.

Amelia steps out on the balcony and hands me a glass. I take a drink and recognize the burn immediately, Tennessee Mule. She sits next to me with the same drink. It's been one of those fucking months.

First, two thugs try to kidnap Amelia, and, in the process, I have to shoot and kill the bastards. She then finds out that I'm a police officer before I can be honest with her, and the horrible shit I did. And then my ex bust out her windows and destroy her car, forcing her to get another one, and now this. Next, my ex kills my mother, and now, she's after Annabelle and me. I think I covered everything. Fuck!

"Annabelle was exhausted, so I laid her down in the crib. I think she had a long day as well."

"Yeah, you can say that again. But, unfortunately, this has been more of a fucked-up day."

"Yes, well, I always believe things happen for a reason. We are being taught a lesson. It's up to us to listen."

"Do you really believe that?" I genuinely ask her.

"Yes, absolutely. God wouldn't put anything on us we couldn't handle. Your mother sacrificed herself to protect you and Annabelle. At the end of the day, she knew her time was coming, and she wanted to make sure her family was taken care of. Like losing my parents, they ensured Lily and I were taken care of before they died. They didn't want us to suffer. Little did they know that their killers were psychos trying to hurt their daughters later in life, but I think they were there with my sister when she was kidnapped. She became a cop to be able to take care of herself and me, which leads to the next statement." Amelia takes a deep breath and continues, "I understand why you kept the truth from me; I just don't understand why you couldn't trust me enough to tell me. Did you think I would blow your cover? Because I can tell you one thing, I know all too well about police work. My sister, brother-in-law, and best friend are all cops. I just wish you had more faith in me."

I get up, completely frustrated that we have to go through this shit all over again. I literally just found out my mother was killed. Is she fucking serious about this shit right now? I put my drink down on the end table and kneel before her, placing my hands in hers. "Baby, please listen to me, and listen to me good. You and Annabelle are all I have. If I lost either one of you, my life would be over. You have to believe me. I really thought I was doing the right thing by not telling you I was a cop undercover. I was involved in so much bad shit, and I didn't want to bring that into your life. I gave up my career to protect the ones I love. I've started from the bottom, and I'm determined to get back on my feet. That's why I went back to school and why I moved here. I never thought I would meet someone who would mean anything to me, let alone change my world completely. I love you, Amelia, and I promise I will give my life protecting you. I just got a lot of shit going on right now. My mother meant everything to me, and Tyra knew that. It's taking everything in my being not to track her down and murder her myself. You are keeping me humble right now. I just need you. Like really need you." I put my head down on her lap, and I feel her rub my head with her fingers. She lifts my face up to look into my eyes.

"I never questioned your love for me. I just wish you could have been honest with me."

"Goddamit Amelia, what will it take for me to get you to trust me again? What?" I spit out in frustration.

"I wasn't finished," shit. "What I was going to say is, that was a month ago. So I'm letting it go. I will protect you and Annabelle as much as you would protect me. I love you too, and we will get through this. Trust me. And no, we're not tracking your ex down and murdering her in the streets. What would your mother think of you then?"

"My mother would kick my ass," rolling my eyes. "I trust you with my life. And I know you will do everything in your power to protect Annabelle as well."

She pulls me closer to her and kisses me with determination and passion I never felt from her before. She pours her heart out into this kiss, and she gives me every bit of her.

I pull her in my arms and lift her up, carrying her into the house, and then into the bedroom. I lay her on the bed gently, and just absorb her completely. Climbing on top of her, I take her soft lips into mine, and she tastes of whiskey and ginger. I make love to her mouth and give her all of me in this kiss. I pour my heart out to her, and I want her to know she means everything to me. She pulls up my shirt and rubs her soft, delicate hands all over my chest and back. She then reaches down and undo my belt and zips my pants down. Next, she reaches inside my boxers and finds my dick growing to full mass. She pushes me off of her, and I roll on my back. She then straddles me with her legs and pushes my pants down to my knees. Finally, she bends down and takes my dick inside her mouth.

"Fuck, Amelia!" She wraps her plump lips around my dick and sucks hard. "Shit, baby. Not so hard. Go slowly." She listens to my instructions and sucks on me softly. "Baby, think of him like an ice cream cone, full of your favorite flavor." She understands and goes to work, like a pro. "Oh my god. That feels so good. Yes, just like that, baby." She continues to lick and suck and nip at my head. She then takes me all the way down her throat, and I almost explode in her mouth.

"Fuck Amelia, you keep doing that, and I'm going to come in that pretty little mouth of yours."

"I want you to come in my mouth. I want to taste you. I never did this before and I want to experience it with you." Jesus, that confession alone makes me want to claim her mouth as mine. I shove my fingers into her curly hair and push further into her mouth. She stops me, wanting to take control of herself.

She takes me in and out, and I feel my balls tightening up. My dick swells in her mouth, and I empty every bit of my cum inside her mouth.

"Fuck baby." She laps up every spill and swallows all of me. She's so fucking hot right now, and I'm so fucking hard all over again.

"Your turn." I roll her over on her back and lift her sundress up. I pull her black lace panties down, and I lick and suck on her clit. She instantly falls apart and gives me all of her essences within seconds. Then, she arches her back off the bed and forces me to go deeper with my tongue, inserting two fingers into her warm pussy.

"Bradley, please."

"What do you want, baby?"

"I want to feel you inside of me. Please, Bradley. I need you." I love it when she begs for me.

I drop my pants and realize I don't have a condom on me. "Fuck!"

"What's wrong, babe?"

"I don't have any condoms. With all the shit going on, I forgot to get some."

"Babe, it's okay. I have condoms in the nightstand."

"You do?"

"Yes, my sister always taught me to keep my own just in case. I'm not sure if they fit you, but we can try."

I reach inside the drawer, and she's right, they will be super tight, but it will have to do for now. "Thanks, babe. It will do for now."

I open the foil and push the condom over my dick. It's small, but it will have to work. I need her pussy now.

I then get on top of her and rub my dick over her clit. She physically shakes at the anticipation. Finally, I enter her walls, and the warmth and tightness are enough to bring me over the edge.

I thrust in and out, picking up speed because it feels so damn good. She's made for my dick, and I can't get enough of her.

"Fuck baby, you feel so good."

"God, yes, please harder. I want to feel you in my stomach."

I pick up the speed and fuck the shit out of her. I think we both wanted it and needed it hard and rough tonight. We both fuck each other like bunnies, and I don't want it to end. I feel her tense around my dick, and I know she's about to come all over this dick.

"Shit, Bradley, I'm coming."

"Yes, baby, give it to me. I want to feel you come."

"I want to feel you too. Please come with me." And just like that, my dick reacts to her command."

"Fucking Jesus." I'm coming so hard and so much, I feel myself spill over the condom.

"Shit!" I try to pull out, but she's clinching me so hard through her orgasm.

"Baby, I'm spilling over. You have to let me go."

"What?"

"My cum, it's spilling over the condom."

"Oh, I'm sorry." She then stops her death grip on my dick, and I pull out.

"I think it's too late. Amelia, fuck, my bad. I should have known better than this. Fuck."

"Bradley, it's okay. Mistakes happen."

"Yeah, but this is a life-altering mistake."

"I know, but what did I say earlier. God will put nothing on us we couldn't handle. I got on the shot the other day. I know it's too early, but we have to have faith that whatever happens is meant to be."

"How can you be so calm about this?" I ask incredulously.

"I've been faced with death several times in my life already. I've learned to live life as God would want me to live it, and you should do the same. We love each other, and if God wants us to be parents together, we will be parents. You don't have to be afraid that you will go through the same thing you've been through before. You must take that experience and learn from it. Okay?"

"Say it again."

"Say what?"

"Say you love me, again."

She stares into my eyes with hope and strength in her gaze. She places her small hands on each side of my face, making sure I hear her. "I love you Bradley."

"How did I get so lucking with you?" wrapping my arms around her waist.

"I think it was meant to be." I then crush my lips on hers and take what I crave the most, affection. I then clean myself up in the bathroom, throwing the condom in the trash. Finally, I get back in bed with her and wrap my arms around her waist, pulling her closer to me.

"You would look sexy as hell carrying my child."

"You think? I won't look like a wobbling whale?" we both laugh.

"Of course, you won't because you will have a piece of me growing inside of you, and Annabelle will have a brother or a sister to play with."

"Yeah, I guess you're right. I thank God every day for having a sibling."

I kiss her on her hair, and we drift off to sleep listening to Annabelle soft snores on the monitor.

CHAPTER 12

AMELIA

I hear the birds chirping and feel the warm sun rays glistening on my skin. I smell Bradley's cologne all over me, and it brings me back to the memories of last night. His touch, his taste impales my thoughts and senses, and I desire even more of him. But then I hear cooing and giggling on the monitor, and it pulls me out of my early morning daydream.

I roll over, and Bradley is fast asleep, so I let him sleep. Then, I get up, put a robe on, and head to the nursery. I look down in the crib and find Annabelle sitting up playing with her stuffed animals.

"Oh my, you're sitting up, baby girl. Yes, you are. Oh, my goodness. You are growing up so much." I pick her up, and we head to the kitchen. "We have to make daddy some breakfast. He had a long day yesterday. Yes, he did." I really believe she understands me because she giggles after I speak.

I sit her down in her highchair and give her toys to play with while making breakfast. I put on some soft music as not to wake Bradley. He needs his rest. He's been through so much lately.

"Hum, what should it be this morning?" After contemplating what I should make, I settle on making a broccoli and ham frittata. It's fast and easy to make, and boy does it taste good.

I grab the cast iron skillet and put it on the stove. I turn the oven to five hundred degrees. I oil the pan and pull out fresh broccoli, sliced ham, bell peppers, cheese, and eggs.

I start to dice up the veggies on the cutlery board and grab a frying pan out of the cabinet. I turn on the stove and place the veggies in the frying pan with olive oil. I sprinkle a dash of seasoning and begin sautéing the veggies; finally, I start slicing the ham into small little dice shapes. I toss the ham in the frying pan as well. Once done, I pour the veggies into the cast iron pan and then pour the whipped eggs over it. I put the skillet in the oven and sprinkle cheese on top to hold the frittata together. I then let it broil for about ten minutes.

I put on a pot of coffee and sit a little to play with Annabelle. "Hey, baby girl. Are you ready to eat?" She shakes her toy as if saying yes. "Okay, what are we going to have today?" I grab bananas and cherries this morning and her oatmeal cereal. I mix it up a little and put it to the side. The frittata should be done by now, so I pull it out of the oven. "Perfect."

I set it on the stove and cover it up. I then get Annabelle food and feed her while waiting for her daddy to wake up.

"Annabelle, I have a question for you? Do you think I'll be a good mother?" She continues to eat and coo in between her bites. "I mean, like really be a good mother. I want to be just like my mom. She read me bedtime stories, kissed me on the forehead, and told me everything would be okay. When I fell off my bike, she was right there to help me back up. When I had my heart broken by Harry Moore, she told me I would find my prince charming, and he would sweep me off my feet just like my daddy did her. So, I waited, and I waited for my prince charming to arrive, and I think I've found him."

"So, you found your prince charming, huh?" I nearly jump out of my skin when I hear Bradley's deep voice.

I turn around, and he's standing there in grey sweatpants hanging from his hips, showing off his physic with no shirt. I see his substantial chest and flat stomach, and I nearly fall off the stool. "Um, yes. Annabelle and I were just talking about my mom."

"Oh really?" He approaches me with lust in his beautiful grey eyes, and I feel butterflies all in my stomach.

"Uh, yes."

"It smells good in here," placing a soft kiss on my forehead and then on Annabelle's, he sits.

"I made ham and broccoli frittata. It's on the stove. Here, I will get you some," I begin to stand, but he pulls me back down.

"No, sit. You made breakfast; I can serve it." So I sit back down and continue to feed Annabelle.

"Bradley?"

"Yes, baby?"

"Do you want to head to Jacksonville today?" I see the muscles in his back tense up at the question.

"Actually, yeah, I do. I need to settle my mother's affairs. She was precise in what she wanted." After a short pause, "Baby?"

"Yes?"

"Can you come with me? I don't think I can do this alone," shocked that he even had to ask. I wasn't going to let him do this alone.

"Of course, I will. We can leave after we eat breakfast."

"Thank you."

"No need to thank me. We're in this together." He serves me a slice of Frittata and a cup of coffee, just how I like it. He then sits next to me.

"I really think she has grown fond of you."

"I hope so because I have of her."

"I can see. You're the first woman other than her mother who has really been around her like this, well, except for the babysitter, that is. I tried not to bring different women in her life."

"If you don't mind me asking, how many women have you've been with since your ex?"

"I don't mind at all. I've been with four other women besides you. They wanted more from me, but I wasn't ready to give more. I actually was very cold to them, and they really didn't deserve it."

"Why me then?"

"Well, when I first saw you in Miami at Ryan's vacation home, I couldn't keep my eyes off you. You were and still are the most beautiful woman I've ever seen or really paid attention to. There was something about your eyes and long beautiful hair, and when you opened your mouth to speak, I was hooked. I just didn't say anything because I wanted to get my shit together before I approached you. But, when I saw you again at the park running, it was like God himself, placed you in my arms, and that was my opportunity to see you again. I couldn't let the opportunity disappear, again."

"Wow, I had no idea. That's the most beautiful thing anyone has ever said to me."

"You deserve so much more than I can give you, but I will spend the rest of my days trying to give you the world." I start to blush because that was basically straight out of a Hallmark movie. I've always thought that type of love or romance never existed. Fortunately, I think I'm wrong. Finally, I found my Prince Charming.

After breakfast and getting dressed, we switched to Bradley's SUV. He wanted to travel in his car because it would be more spacious.

We're now on I-95, heading south to Jacksonville.

"So, baby, what about you? How many men have you dated?" Out of the blue, he starts asking me questions, and I don't mind because I have nothing to hide.

"I've dated three guys while in school. They were okay, but I'm pretty sure they were after only one thing that I could not and would not give. My mom always told me my body was a temple, and I shouldn't let just anyone touch it, let alone enter it. Besides, if you want the prize, you need to at least take a girl out on a proper date, geez."

"So, why me?"

"Well, you're right about one thing, we have a connection like no other. When you first touched me, I felt this electricity run through my body and explode in my stomach. It was a feeling I'd never felt before with anyone else. I took it as a sign from my parents that you belonged in my life. I didn't care that you had a daughter or even a past. I knew I wanted you. Then, you stepped through that door like a model on a magazine with a baby girl in your hands, and I thought that was the sexiest thing I've ever seen. You stood six foot five with a chest of a God and an ass of a statue. Beautiful eyes that would take the soul of every girl, and I was the one you couldn't stop looking at. At first, I was a little nervous, but once you came back into my life, I knew then that it was meant to be."

"Wow, now that's something I wasn't expecting to hear. I thought my daughter would be a turnoff, so that's why I stayed away."

"It was quite the opposite. I love kids; as you can see, I have a niece and two nephews, and another nephew on the way. I love kids, and Annabelle is absolutely adorable. She will win the hearts of anyone she's around."

"Yeah, that's what I'm afraid of. I'll have to break the legs of every guy who tries to kiss her." We both start laughing.

"Shhh. Annabelle is sleeping in the back," I hush him, still giggling.

"Oh, don't worry about that. She can sleep through a freight train passing through the house."

"Right."

"So, you thought I was hot, huh?" waggling his eyebrows.

"Prince Charming, himself!" swooning to the thought of his hands drifting across my body.

~

We arrive at the hospital where Bradley's mother spent her last moments on this earth. She's finally at peace and doesn't have to worry about the pains of the world any longer.

I get Annabelle from the back seat while Bradley gets her stroller. I can feel the tension in his demeanor, so I rub his back to soothe him a little. He places Annabelle in the stroller, and I grab her backpack I put together before we left. We then enter the hospital like we're already a family.

"Good morning, Ma'am. I'm Bradley Philips, here to claim my mother's body, Mrs. Dorothy Philips."

"Awe, yes. Do you have an ID?"

"Yes, ma'am. Here you go." Bradley reaches in his back pocket to get his wallet out and pulls his ID out to give to the lady behind the desk.

"Thank you, right this way. We're terribly sorry for your loss. Mrs. Philips was such a breath of fresh air."

"Thank you. That she was," Bradley agrees.

We're taken down to the morgue, where Mrs. Philips is sitting on a slab in a cooler to preserve her body. I've been in this type of room a couple of times, and it never sits right with me. I hate coming to the morgue, but for Bradley, I will be his rock; he's going to need me.

The mortician pulls out the tray with his mother lying peacefully, and Bradley instantly breaks, falling to his knees; earth-shattering cries spilling from his lips, and all I can do is wrap my arms around his large frame and hold on to him for dear life.

"It will be okay," I whisper in his ear. "She's okay now. She's in a better place now. Her spirit is no longer suffering, and you must stay strong; let it all out. I'm here. Use me for strength." He continues to rock back and forth a bit longer, sobs escaping from his lips, before he speaks.

"Did you find out how she died?" And I knew exactly what he was asking.

"Yes, the mortician has the full report. Come with me; I will find a quiet place for you and your family," the nurse escorts us.

Bradley stands with my assistance, holding me close to him. I push Annabelle in her stroller while she's sleeping. The receptionist takes us to a quiet room to mourn the loss of his mother.

"I thought when this day would come, I would be stronger and glad she no longer has to suffer, but this right here hurts so fucking much," he starts to breathe harder, and I'm pretty sure he's starting to hyperventilate.

"Baby, please slow your breathing. Here, follow me. Take a deep breath in and slowly let it out through your nose. Take a deep breath in and slowly let it out." He's following my commands and starts to physically relax. "That's it. You're doing great."

"Why does it hurt so much? Why?"

"Because you loss a part of you. Your mother meant everything to you, and there's no replacing her. You will have to learn how to live without her in this world but remember she's always here in your heart and in Annabelle's heart," placing my hand over his chest where his heart resides, giving him the comfort he craves.

"Thank you, Amelia. I don't know if I could've done this without you," tears streaming down our cheeks, I wrap my arms around his shoulders and continue to rock him back and forth. A soothing embrace is all I can give him in this moment.

About ten minutes later, the mortician walks in.

"Hi, I'm Dr. Litterman. I'm truly sorry for your loss."

"Thank you," Bradley responds dully.

"I have the report here. It appears that your mother died from suffo-cation. She had markings around her mouth and nose that signified handprints. We sent the report to the local police department to start an investigation." Bradley drops his head into his hands and starts shaking his head aggressively, once again. One nightmare after another.

"This can't be true! This can't be happening! How could she do this? How could she take my mother away from me?" I know precisely what Bradley is referring to, but the doctor has no idea.

"Do you know who did this?" asks Dr. Litterman.

"We think we do?" I answer for Bradley.

"You must go to the police right away. They will want to know."

"We will, and thank you for your help. We appreciate it."

He then nods his head and walks out quietly.

"That fucking bitch!" Bradley says through clenched teeth. "I'm going to kill that heartless bitch," seething through every venomous word.

"Bradley, baby. Please. We can't be certain that she's the one who did this?"

"Who the fuck else would take my mother's life without a fucking care in the fucking world? That bitch tried to take my daughter out, and now she has killed my mother. She will pay. She will fucking pay!" I see the hate and pain in his eyes. Flames blazing on the surface, ready to pour out into the world. He's pacing the room with clenched fist. His veins popping out, and for the first time, I'm afraid of what he might do.

"Bradley, baby, please calm down," I beg with all the sincerity I can muster up.

"Fuck that! I've done everything for that bitch. I was building a life with her, and she fucks it all up. All this time, I thought it was my fault. But this is not my fault. No, this is hers, and she will pay. She will get what's coming to her," I cringe at every word spilled from his seething tone. I've never seen him this teed off.

Annabelle starts crying and wants to be picked up. So, I unfasten her belt and bring her to my chest. I then rock her in my arms and soothe her. I look into her eyes, and she has the same beautiful eyes like her daddy, misty grey. "It's okay, sweetie. Everything will be okay."

Bradley then stops pacing suddenly and drops down on the couch in front of me. He places his head into my lap like he wants to be consoled as well. While I rock Annabelle in my arms, I glide my small hand over his soft waves, and he starts to weep to himself once more.

I find myself soothing the two most influential people in my life right now, Bradley and Annabelle. They need my support and my affection, and I vow to give it to them.

CHAPTER 13

BRADLEY

I wake up to an unfamiliar place. White walls surround me and white linen on the bed. I hear water splashing outside as if I'm near an ocean or a lake. I smell fresh cotton in the air and a taste of salt on my tongue. Adjusting my eyes to the light, I get up abruptly because I can't remember how I got here.

"Annabelle? Amelia?"

I scramble to my feet and almost lose my balance. What the fuck is wrong with me? I steady myself and head for the door to the bedroom. I open it up, and I enter what looks like an executive suite of a hotel. There's modern furniture of soft greys and light blue accents. A sofa and loveseat near the balcony bay window and a small dining table near the full kitchen. There are stainless steel appliances and earthly paintings on the wall. I hear laughing from my side, and I turn in that direction. There's another door, so I head towards it. I open it and find Annabelle in Amelia's arms, laughing and giggling. My racing heart slows a notch, and my thoughts come rushing back to me.

I claimed my mother's body, and I remember a doctor speaking to me about how she died. I had a strong feeling Tyra was responsible for killing my mother so she could find Annabelle and me. Amelia calmed me down, and that's all I remember of that horrific day.

"Hey," I say to Amelia.

"Oh, hi, babe. We didn't wake you, did we? I tried to be as quiet as possible so you can get some rest."

"Oh, no, but everything is a blur. How did we get here? Where are we?"

"You were really upset, so Dr. Litterman gave you a mild sedative to calm you down. He suggested we get a hotel instead of trying to drive back home just in case you had a reaction to the medication. So, I checked us in a hotel near Jacksonville Beach."

"How did you get me up here?"

"It definitely wasn't easy. You're a heavy man and trying to carry Annabelle at the same time, my gosh. People thought I kidnapped you," she snickers to herself.

"My bad, babe. I don't know what to say."

"Don't say anything. And you have nothing to be sorry for. We're in this together," I nod my head slightly, feeling a throbbing sensation. "Are you hungry?" summoned on cue, my stomach starts to growl. "I guess I have my answer. I will order room service. What do you have a taste for?"

"Isn't room service a little expense?"

"I can afford it, remember. So don't worry about the cost. And please stop with the chivalry act. Sometimes, I can pay for things as well."

"Not, if I'm around. You're my responsibility, not the other way around."

"Cut the shit. I don't believe in that and never have. If I want to spend my money on us, then I will, and there's nothing you can do or say to change my mind. Do I make myself clear?" Amelia clearly standing her ground.

Putting me in my place never looked sexier than coming from this woman right here. "Crystal."

"So, steak or fish?"

"Fish."

"Fish it is. Coming right up." She walks over to the phone and calls for room service.

"Hi, can I order two servings of fish and veggies, one with sautéed potatoes and a bottle of Riesling?" There's a pause, and then she hangs up.

"It will be here in thirty minutes. I already fed and bathed Annabelle."

"What time is it?" unaware of anything at this point.

"It's one in the afternoon. I scheduled an appointment to meet the detective at three today. He will be coming to us."

"Wow, I don't know what to say?"

"Babe, you don't have to say anything. I told you, I got your back. You would do the same for me if the roles were reversed. For once, you can depend on someone else instead of everyone depending on you."

She's right about that. I've always been the source of income, support, nurture, and protection. It's time for me to accept a little help once in a while.

"I love you, Amelia."

"I love you, babe," reaching up and placing a kiss on my cheek. How did I get so luck? "Do you want some water? You must be dehydrated from all the meds and sleep."

"Yeah, I'm a little parched."

She hands Annabelle to me, and I take her in my arms. Amelia then walks to the kitchen area.

"Hey, daddy's girl. How's my pumpkin? Are you having fun with Amelia? You like her, don't you? I like her too, and one day I'm going to marry her. I feel it in my bones."

Amelia comes back into the bedroom. "Dinner is here," handing me a bottle of water.

Downing the water within seconds, I must've been very dehydrated.

"Okay." We all walk to the dining area, and we sit down. I put Annabelle on my knee while I eat. "This is really good. Thanks, babe. It's just what I needed."

"Yes, it is, and you are certainly welcome."

"No, I mean, thank you for everything. You have truly been a godsend in my life and Annabelle's."

"And you have in mine," smiling with adoration in her eyes, Amelia continues to finish her meal.

~

We're heading back to Savannah when I receive a phone call from my mother's lawyer. Hell, I didn't even know she had a lawyer.

"Hello, is this Bradley Philips?" the man asks.

"Yes, this is he. How can I help you?"

"I'm your mother's attorney. I was trying to catch you before you left Jacksonville but got held up in court. I have some paperwork to go over with you. Your mother had a Will drawn up years ago, and I would like to go over it with you."

"We're on our way back to Savannah. Do we need to turn back around? We're not that far away."

"If you can, it's crucial that we meet in person."

"Okay, we'll turn around."

"My office is located just before you get to Saint John's Town Center. I will send you the address in a few."

"Okay, thank you, uh...I didn't catch your name."

"It's Maurice White."

"Thanks, Mr. White. We'll be there shortly."

I then hang up the phone.

"What's going on?" Amelia asks.

"Apparently, my mother had a Will I knew nothing about, and her lawyer would like to discuss it with me. He prefers that we meet in person."

"Okay. Yeah, they did the same thing when my parents died. They had to meet us in person. I guess because of confidentiality."

"Yes, he has to make sure he's speaking with the right person."

"Do you want me to go in with you?"

"Of course. You keep me calm when I want to cause mass destruction."

"Your guardian angel at your service."

We pull up to the address, and I take a deep breath. It can't get any worse, can it? Amelia grabs my hand and squeezes it. "You can do this." I look into her eyes for support and comfort. She's definitely been my rock through all of this. We get out of the car and walk into the office. It reminds me of any other lawyer's office, books everywhere on bookshelves, lobby chairs against the floor-length windows, and graduate degrees and certificates on the wall. We walk up to the receptionist's desk.

"Hi, can I help you?" the receptionist asks.

"Yes, we have an appointment with Mr. White."

"Okay, you can have a seat over there. I will let him know you're here."

"Thank you." I grab Amelia's hand and escort her to the chairs. She has Annabelle on her hip. She's really good with her. If I didn't know any better, she would remind me of a loving mother to Annabelle already.

After a few minutes, Mr. White comes out of his office to greet us. He stands five foot nine, slightly overweight, with a nice-looking suit. "Hello, Mr. Philips. I'm Mr. White, your mother's attorney. I'm really sorry for your loss. She was a wonderful soul inside and out," offering his hand, I take it, giving him a firm shake.

"This is Amelia and my daughter, Annabelle."

"Ah, yes, the famous Annabelle. Your mother was very fond of her granddaughter."

"How long have you known my mother?"

"Since you were a kid. You used to sit in those very chairs and play with your video game while I met with your mother. She was very protective of you."

"Wow, I don't remember that at all."

"It was a long time ago. Have a seat while I get the documents."

We sit down and wait in silence.

"Here we are." Mr. White walks back in with a file in his hands. "Your mother set a trust fund for Annabelle for when she turns eighteen years old."

"For how much? My mother never had that kind of money."

"Actually, she did. She inherited a lump sum of money from your grandparents. The trust fund is in the amount of five hundred thousand."

"What?" I spit out, astounded at the amount. We never had money like that. This is crazy.

"Yes, and there's more. Your mother left you everything else, the property, her assets, and her inheritance."

"I'm so confused. How, where, wha—?"

"Please, Mr. Philips, let me continue. I know this is a lot to take in, but just let me finish." Amelia rubs my shoulder to comfort me, and I nod my head for him to continue, feeling a wave of calmness through her touch.

"The total amount is in the sum of two hundred-fifty million dollars. Once you sign the documents, I will have everything signed over to you and your daughter. The only request that your mother has is, if you have any more children, to start a trust for them as well. She wants her grandchildren to be well taken care of."

"Why didn't she tell me any of this?" I shake my head violently.

"I think she wanted to protect you. Your father was very abusive towards her, and she ran away from him and moved here. She felt that if she lived a simple life, your father would never find you and take you away from her."

"What the fuck are you talking about?" no longer having control of my emotions or the fucked-up shit that comes out of my mouth.

"I know this is a lot to take in, but you must understand that your mother did everything in your best interest. She cared for you dearly."

"I can't believe this shit."

"Baby, it will be okay."

"How? My entire life has been a fucking joke. A fucking lie. My ex was a fucking psycho, and two assholes just tried to kill you just the other day. This is all so fucked up. I can't—I just can't right now." I get up and storm out of the office, leaving Amelia and Annabelle to deal with the rest of that shit.

"Mrs. Philips, please have him sign these and get them back to me."

"Okay, I will." I hear Amelia say to the lawyer before I storm out of the building. I kneel down and put my head in between my legs and take a deep breath. This shit is really fucked-up, like bat-shit crazy fucked-up.

How do I not remember any of this?

Did I really block out everything when I was a kid?

Why didn't she tell me my father abused her?

Why didn't she tell me anything? I demand the fucking gods.

I hear Annabelle crying and Amelia trying to soothe her, and at that moment, I understand why my mother kept it all from me. She wanted to protect me. She tried to shelter me from all the evil and hate given by that wicked fucktard. I would do the same for Annabelle in a heartbeat.

Amelia comes rushing out of the office with Annabelle in her arms. I grab her by the arm and bring them both into my chest, and I hold them. After, what seemed forever, I push away and force Amelia to look into my eyes. Her hazel eyes inspiring me to want more out of life, to do better. Ryan saw something in me that day, and I want to prove him right.

"Let's go."

"Hold on, babe. You need to sign these in order to receive your inheritance."

"What do you think I should do?"

"I think you should sign them. Your mother spent her entire life trying to protect you, and this is her gift to you and Annabelle. I think you should honor her wishes and take the money and do something good with it." I take the folder out of her hand. She hands me a pen, and I sign the documents my mother kept from me for so long to protect me.

"Here's the keys. I have to give these back to Mr. White."

"Okay babe; oh, and babe?"

"Yeah?" I turn around.

"You won't regret this."

"I know." I head back inside to give the folder to the receptionist.

"Can I get a copy of the documents, please?"

"Of course. Wait here; I will be right back."

A few minutes later, she returns with my copies.

"Thank you."

"You're welcome, Mr. Philips. Have a wonderful day."

"You do the same."

"Mr. Philips, hold on. I forgot to give you this. It's a letter from your mother. It may have the answers you're looking for."

I take the letter and stick into my coat pocket. I'm going to need a drink before I even try to comprehend this letter. The final words of my dearest mother.

I then walk to the car. Now, I just need to find Tyra crazy-ass before she harms herself or anyone else. So I get in the car, and we head back to Savannah, thankful to never have to return to my childhood home, again.

CHAPTER 14

AMELIA

*I*t has been a weird couple of months for all of us, but we managed to get through it unscathed. Bradley and Annabelle have adjusted very well at my home. I know it's really soon to move a guy and his daughter into my home, but I felt like it was the right thing to do under the circumstances. There was no way I could leave him and Annabelle in his house while his ex was still out there. Besides, the crazy bitch knows where I live as well. So it's best that Bradley and I stick together rather than be a part.

Daphne, the babysitter, agreed to continue watching Annabelle while Bradley and I went back to work. I arrive at the café, and Dianella pulls up simultaneously.

"Hey, Dianella," I say as we get out of our cars.

"Hi, stranger, it's been a while. Is everything okay? We haven't seen you in a couple of months."

"Oh, yeah. It's been crazy, but we're okay," keeping the truth from her. No need to worry her too…right?

"We?" Well, so much for that. She can always see right through my bullshit…

"Yes, Bradley, Annabelle, and I. They're staying at my house until Tyra is located."

"Are you sure you want to do that? You barely know him."

"Yes, of course. I would never leave a person stranded. You know that. Where is this coming from?" I question as she opens the front door of the café, and I turn the alarm off.

"Never mind. Forget I said anything. I'm just worried. That's all."

"You have nothing to worry about. Bradley is a perfect guy; he's just going through a lot right now. He just lost his mother, found out his father was abusing his mother, and his ex-girlfriend, who is the mother of his daughter, may be responsible for killing his mother. Oh, and two guys tried to kidnap me, and Bradley had to kill them both to protect me, which by the way, I'm forever grateful for that," I confess as she turns on all the lights, and we head to the back to start baking.

"Holy shit Amelia!" stopping in her tracks. "I had no idea. Why didn't you tell me? I would've been there for you or did something, anything."

"It happened so fast, I'm still trying to wrap my head around it all, catch up sort of speak, and I need to watch my back for psycho ex."

"What are you going to do?" she asks with genuine concern in her tone.

"Jason has placed the house on extra patrol for the past couple of weeks. We haven't seen any signs of her since that day in the park, but I'm pretty sure she will grace us with her presence soon. It's only a matter of time."

"Amelia, please be careful. You know what happened last year. Both Kim and Lily had us scared. I don't want the same thing to happen to you."

"I know. We will be. Did I tell you Bradley is a cop from Jacksonville?"

"Hell no, you didn't tell me that!"

"Yeah, he was undercover for a while, and that was part of his decision to move here once he brought down an entire drug and sex trafficking ring."

"Shit, this dude got a lot of shit going on."

"And he just found out that he's now a millionaire. So, like, he's worth more than me."

"Shit."

"Hey, stop saying shit."

"What the fuck else should I say? This is a lot to lay on a person. Is he mentally, okay?"

"I think so, but he has been angrier than anything lately." We both put on our aprons and wash our hands.

"Can you blame him? His entire life has been a lie and turned upside down. I would be angry too."

"Yeah, I know. I try to soothe him as much as possible, but I don't know how much I can take. You know?"

"All you can do is be there for him in this time of need. Do you have a picture of this ex?"

"Shit, I was meaning to ask, but it slipped my mind."

"So, you mean to tell me, there's a psycho on the loose, and you don't even know how she looks? This just gets better and better," she smirks with laughter.

"Well, it's been a lot going on. I think I saw her in my garage, but we can't be certain. I will ask for it tonight," beating myself up for making such a stupid mistake. I know better than this.

"You need to. For all we know, she's been coming to the café, around the house, and you don't even know how she looks."

"Okay, okay. I will get it," I spit out in frustration.

"Look, Amelia. I'm not trying to piss you off. I...just—"

"Looking out for my best interest. I know."

We then start preparing the loaves of bread, pastries, and coffee cakes. Dianella is really good at this. I don't know why she isn't going to culinary school instead of nursing school. This is her passion.

"I really don't understand why you haven't gone to culinary school. I watch you sometimes, and you're so peaceful when you bake in the morning. Hell, it's calming my anxiety as we speak."

"Actually, I started taking evening classes."

"Seriously?"

"Yes, I'm still doing nursing school, but during the summer, I'm taking lessons for cooking."

"Holy shoot. That's great. I'm so happy for you."

"Yeah, Lenny encouraged me to follow my dream."

"Wow, you two are getting pretty serious."

"I know, very shocking, but I like him. You remember when you told me how you felt when Brad comes around you?"

"Yeah, it's the most amazing feeling in the world. Like everything is at a standstill, and we're moving in sync."

"That's how it feels with Lenny and me sometimes. I want what you, Lily, my brother, Ryan, and Kim have. I want that type of love, and I think I've found it too."

"Oh my gosh. I'm so happy for you, Dianella. You deserve happiness. We both do."

"Yes, we do. Now let's finish up before we be serving bread and water for breakfast." We both burst out laughing and start creating masterpieces with baked goods.

~

I walk into the house and find Annabelle and Bradley playing on the floor. I smell something delicious cooking on the stove, and I see a tall glass of wine waiting for me.

"Hey, baby. How was work?" Bradley asks from the floor.

"It was good. We had a lot of customers today, but then again, we always have a lot of customers. It felt good to finally go back to work. What smells so good?"

"I'm making you bell peppers stuffed with homemade shrimp fried rice."

"Umm, sounds delicious. How was work for you?"

"I finally closed the biggest account I've ever had, making my clients millions, which gives me thousands in commission."

"Sound like we have something to celebrate." He stands up and picks Annabelle up in his arms. He then twirls her around, and she starts giggling uncontrollably.

"We also have something else to celebrate."

"Oh, what's that?" fidgeting with anticipation while I sip my wine.

"My inheritance just transferred into my account, and we're now millionaires."

I start laughing, "Babe, we were always millionaires."

"That's not the same. I don't want you ever spending your money again."

I put my hand on my hip, ready to argue.

"Wait, just hear me out," shutting my mouth, waiting to hear his explanation. But, instead, he walks over to me with Annabelle in his arms.

"Baby, please sit." I do as he says. "Annabelle and I have been talking, and we decided that we want you a part of our family." I gasp and put my hand over my mouth, waiting for the words to come alive. "We've loved you since the moment we saw you. You are kind, loving, and you are a beautiful soul inside and out. You brighten both our lives and have brought warmth into our hearts when we least expected it. You were willing to give us everything when we needed you the most, and we will forever be thankful to have someone like you in our lives. Annabelle and I have been through a lot, and so have you, but together, we can conquer the world." He bends down on one knee with Annabelle sitting on the other. He reaches into his pocket and pulls out a small box. I feel tears spilling from my eyes and running down my cheeks, and my lips are trembling with joy. "Amelia Matthews, baby, will you do us the honor of being my wife." He opens the little box, and it has the most beautiful diamond I've ever seen. It's glistening in the light, and colors of the rainbow shine all over the room.

I stop breathing and time passes slowly. Every sound is magnified, and my heart beats rapidly in my chest.

"Say yes already!" I turn at the voice of my sisters, Lily and Dianella.

"What—"

"Baby, will you marry me?"

Turning back around, "Oh…yes. Of course," I say through sobbing cries. Bradley reaches for my left hand and places the diamond on my ring finger. I look down at it, and then I look into his eyes. Those gorgeous eyes won me over the first time I met him.

He stands up and wraps his free arm around my waist, lifting me off the floor and smashing his lips to mine. I hear Annabelle giggling on the side of us and cheers ring throughout the house. I pull away for a much-needed breath, breaking one intimate connection.

"How in the world did you pull this off? And you, Dianella. All that shit you were giving me earlier. You knew. Didn't you?"

She shrugs her shoulders, "I still love you, sis."

"Yeah, sure you do." I look at my ring again, totally enchanted by it.

"Honey, Brad came to us a while ago to ask your hand in marriage. We all can tell that y'all are meant to be together, and you deserve to be happy," says Lily with Jasmine in her arms. She gives me a hug of endearment. "I love you, baby girl."

"I love you too, sissy pooh," tears welling up in my eyes.

Dianella then approaches me. "You have no idea how hard it was to keep this a secret from you. When you poured your heart out this morning, I so wanted to tell you then, but I promised to keep my mouth shut. And then when we closed the café up, I was doing like ninety to beat you here. I made it in the nick of time."

We both laugh because we know I can drive fast when I want to. Jason and Ryan then congratulate Bradley, and we all head out to the balcony to have drinks.

"Baby, this is the best gift you and Annabelle could ever give me. I was thirty-eight hot when you told me I shouldn't spend my money on you and Annabelle."

"I know you were; that's why I had to stop you before you cursed me out in front of your whole family," he chuckles. I slap him on the shoulder playfully, and he turns away like I hurt him, "Ouch."

"Oh, please. That little tap did not hurt."

"Oh really." He picks me up off the floor and starts tickling me. I start laughing in a frenzy.

"Babe, please stop. Please. Put me down."

"Are you going to apologize?"

"Apologize, for what?" He then starts tickling me again. "Okay, okay. I apologize. Please." He then put me back down and looks into my eyes.

"Baby, I love you, and I cannot wait to start our lives together as husband and wife."

"I love you too, and I can't wait either." He then kisses me softly with his plump lips. He takes my bottom lip in his mouth and sucks on it. He pulls me closer into him and deepens the kiss, thrusting his tongue in my mouth, exploring, searching, tasting.

"Get a room!" someone shouts, but we ignore them. In this moment, it's only him and me, and I want him so bad my pussy aches for his attention. Instead, he pulls away, and I'm left feeling alone and breathless. Shit, I want him so bad.

"Wait for tonight, baby," he whispers in my ear. "I will give you what you want and more." He then kisses me on the forehead to hold me over until tonight.

"Okay," I say with sadness in my voice.

Everyone is having a good time, Jason turned on some music, and the kids are playing on the floor with their toys. They are getting along so well, future cousins in the making.

After a while, Kim walks up to me and hugs me. Her stomach sticking out now. "I need to talk to you," she whispers in my ear.

"Is everything okay?"

"Yes, I just have some information for you and Brad."

"Okay, let's talk now."

"No, it can wait. Enjoy your engagement party. You deserve it. I love you, sweetie."

"I love you too."

"Shit, this boy is kicking the shit out of me."

"Aren't you due any day now?"

"No, I have another month to go."

"That means nothing. Take it easy. Have a seat."

"Yes, babe, do as she says. You've been doing too much," Ryan pleads with Kim.

"Ouch, fuck, that hurts." Kim doubles down, holding her stomach. I then hear splashing on the floor.

"Kim, honey. It's time. Your water just broke," I announce calmly.

"Shit, we need to go now!" Ryan starts to panic.

"Ryan, calm down. I'm just having a kid, not open-heart surgery. Everything is in the SUV. Just help me get to the car. FFFUUUCC-CKKK. That hurts," Kim screams out.

Ryan lifts Kim into his arms and carries her to the car. We all grab a kid off the floor and follow them. Bradley turns off the stove and sets the alarm, and we all leave for the hospital.

"Baby, do you want anything from the café in the lobby? We're headed there to get a few snacks for everyone," Bradley asks.

"A Red Bull and some fruit will be good."

"Okay, we'll be right back."

Bradley and Jason head to the hospital's café while we wait patiently for Kim to have her baby boy. Of course, we shouldn't have the kids out this late, but none of us want to leave. It's been five hours since we arrived, and we are all exhausted with anticipation and lack of sleep.

I look up because I hear doors open, and I see Ryan walking through. I jump to my feet, and so does Dianella and Lily. "How is she?"

"He's here! Ryan Jacob, the third, has arrived. He's nine pounds and eight ounces. He has all his toes and fingers, and he has a strong set of lungs. Kim is doing great." I can see the joy all over his face, and I automatically fall in love with my nephew, who I haven't even met yet.

"Can we see him?" I ask impatiently.

"Of course, once she and RJ head to their private suite, you all can come in." He then glides back through the doors.

"Oh my gosh. This is such a wonderful day. I'm engaged to a wonderful man, and my best friend just had her first baby," I announce to everyone in earshot with more enthusiasm than I anticipated.

"Yes, we've been very blessed through all our trials and tribulations. We have angels looking over us," Lily admits.

"Yes, we do," Dianella agrees, holding one of the triplets.

Bradley and Jason come back with snacks, and we tell them the good news.

"We can head back in a few, and then we can leave. I know Annabelle is exhausted."

"Okay, baby, whatever you need. I can always take Annabelle back home and come pick you up later."

"No, we came here together. We leave together."

"Okay. We're staying."

Ryan comes back a few minutes later to escort all of us to the back. Policy says no children are allowed, but Ryan donates so much money to the hospital that they overlook that little rule.

We enter the room, and I see Kim holding her baby boy in her arms. I never thought I would see this sight considering she was adamant about not having children. But now I see her, and I know she will do fantastic as a mother.

"Everyone, we've decided to get married right now. We want to be man and wife before we take RJ home."

"Oh my gosh. But wait, how, where?" I ask.

"Right here with all of you here. You guys are all the family I have, and I don't want to do this without any of you here. We're just waiting on Ryan's parents, and then we can get started. They should be here in a few minutes. They have a pastor on call, and he is willing to marry us and file the paperwork with the judge first thing in the morning."

Oh, my gosh, I'm so excited." Lily gushes.

"Aw, my precious grandson. He looks like both of you. He has your eyes Kim and your cheekbones Ryan. You two created a beautiful child," Ryan's mother raves as she walks into the room, arms full of gifts.

"Son, you did a good job," Ryan's father says, patting him on the back. "I'm proud of ya."

We all wait patiently for the pastor to get started. "Are you ready?"

"I've been ready since the day I met her."

"Then, let's not waste another moment. Since this is a brief cere-mony, you can each say your own vows to each other," the pastor states.

"Okay, here goes nothing. Kim, baby, you are my light in the dark, my strength in a fight, and my wisdom in decisions we make for us to thrive in life. We were two lost souls who found each other drifting in the wind, and now we're one and forever. I will love you; I will protect you; I will provide for you; I will encourage you. I will be yours forever."

Kim sobbing from crying when hearing those beautiful words. "Ryan, honey, you are my knight in shiny armor; you are my strength when I need it; you are my breath when I can't breathe. I never wanted love until I found you, and now, I know, I've waited a thousand years for you, and I will wait for even more to be one with you. I love you, and I will support you, and I will uplift you every step of the way."

"With the power vested in me, you may kiss the —" before the pastor could even get the words out, they were kissing with passion and love for a lifetime.

~

We're headed back home after what seemed like a long-drawn-out day. We're all exhausted and finally ready to go to sleep.

Bradley pulls the car into the garage, and we head upstairs. "This has been the best day of my life."

"Oh really?" Bradley wraps his arms around my waist and lifts me up to kiss him on the lips.

"Yes, I'm engaged to a wonderful man; my best friend just had her baby and got married all in the same night. I don't know how it will get any better than this."

"You're about to find out."

I look into his eyes and wonder what he has up his sleeve. I take Annabelle out of his arms and take her to her room. I get her dressed for bed, and I begin rocking her to sleep. She falls quickly. I place her in the crib and turn the monitor on. I then head to the bedroom, and when I walk in, I see white candles lit everywhere. I see white rose petals scattered over the bed, and I hear soft music playing in the background.

Bradley is standing in the middle of the room, and he reaches his hand out, encouraging me to take it.

"Dance with me." I take his hand and let him lead me into a smooth seductive waltz. I sway my hips to the music and let him glide me across the floor. The rhythm of the music takes us away into a romantic private island with just the two of us.

I never knew he could dance so well, which gives me life in my bones. He twirls me, and I spin with perfection into his arms. "I know you love to dance, so I thought I would bring the dance floor to our bedroom."

"Thank you so much. I love it, and I hope to have many more dances with you."

"And you shall."

He picks me up and lays me down on the bed, my hair scattered all around me and my dress raised a little up my thighs. He stands over me and admires every little feature of my body.

"I love your beautiful smooth skin with tiny scars on the surface. I love the color of your eyes, with specks of gold glistening on the shell. I love your long curly hair, with shine and perfection to every strand. I love your soul, so kind and hopeful. I love your heart, so full and giving. I love you, all of you, Amelia, and I want to wake up every morning next to your beautiful body and go to sleep every night staring into your radiant eyes."

I can feel hot tears burning in the back of my eyelids, wanting to break free. I can feel my heart racing with anticipation of what will come next. I can feel my heart fill with love for this beautiful creature. I can feel my body ache for his touch.

"Baby, I love you more than words can express, and I know without a doubt that we will spend the rest of our lives learning and teaching each other who we are and what we want. You are my soulmate, and I want nothing more than to spend my life with you."

"Take off your panties," he demands, and I oblige with every fiber in my being. I slowly slide my panties down my legs and let them drop on the bed.

"Take off your dress." I reach down and pull each side of my dress up over my head, letting my breast bounce free from their hold. I continue to lift the dress over my head and then drop it on the other side of the bed.

"Now, spread your legs and let me see you. All of you." I open my legs wide so he can have a perfect view of my pussy.

"Now, reach down and play with yourself. I want to watch you make yourself come." Fuck, I never masturbated in front of anyone. He notices my hesitation. "Baby, it's just you and me. I want to know everything about you, including how you please yourself."

I take a deep breath. "Okay," I oblige meekly, reaching down feeling for my clit. I can feel the moisture I've built from anticipating arousal, and I smooth silkiness all over my pussy. Then, finally, I close my eyes because it feels so damn good when I touch myself.

"Open your eyes, baby. I want to see your eyes when you come." I flutter my eyes back open and stare into his. He then takes off his shirt, and I get even more aroused. His body is made from the very stone of the gods, and all I want to do is lick it right now; taste the firmness of his body; feel the salty glaze slide down my tongue and heighten every cell in my very being .

I continue to play with myself, and I feel myself getting ready to come. Bradley then takes his pants off and pushes his boxers down his long, muscular legs. His dick stands at attention, and he strokes it with his strong hand. I arch my back off the bed, the pleasure so intense, it's too much pleasure to handle.

"I want to see you come, baby." I insert two fingers in my pussy and penetrate myself over and over again. "Fuck, that's hot, baby."

"Aw, Bradley, I'm about to come."

"That's it, baby, come for me." I feel fire building in my core and electricity slicing through my veins. I feel hot, silky moisture spilling out of me, and I continue to milk it. Bradley drops to his knees and inhales the scent of my cum. "Fuck baby, you smell so fucking good."

I continue to insert my fingers when I feel his tongue lick my pussy. "Shit Bradley, please!"

"Please, what, my love? Tell me what you want," he continues his pleasuring with his delicate, yet firm tongue.

"Please do that again. I want to feel your mouth on my pussy, baby." And just like that, he feasts on my essence and continues to pull my soft silky cream out of me. I buck my hips off the bed, and he uses his strong arms to hold me down, perfectly aligned with his mouth. Then, once he has lapped every bit of me up, he flips me over.

"Get on your knees, baby. I want to make love to you from the back." I do as he says. "Now put your head on the bed and let me see that sexy pussy of yours." I place my head on the bed, and I feel him swipe his tongue over my pussy, and then my ass and I near jump off the bed. He grabs me by the hips and brings me back to him. "Where are you going, my love?"

"Um, nowhere."

"I'm about to fuck you without a condom. Are you okay with that?"

"Yes, Bradley. I'm okay with that."

He then thrusts his dick inside of me and fuck me into the next century. I scream on top of my lungs because it's so intense. "Fuck Amelia, you feel so fucking good."

"Bradley, baby. Yes, baby. That's it. Right there. Please, Bradley. Please harder." He thrust harder and harder, and I immediately explode around his thick dick.

"Fuck, baby. That's it. Give it to me. I want to feel your cum all over this dick."

He continues to milk every bit of me on his dick, and then I feel his dick swell in my pussy. "Shit, I'm about to come, baby. Do you want to have my baby?"

"What—"

"Do you want to have my baby, Amelia?" he thrust into me harder.

"Fuck! Yes, Bradley. I want to have your baby, please." He then releases his load inside me, filling me with so much cum. He continues to pump his seed into me, and I feel it running down my leg.

"Fuck baby, that is so hot. I will always love seeing my seed drip out of that sweet pussy of yours. I love you, baby."

"I love you too." He pulls out of me, and I drop to the bed and roll over. He then gets in beside me and holds me in his arms, not rushing to clean himself up.

"Baby, I was serious about a baby. I would love to have another with you."

"I would be honored to give you a child." He then kisses me on my hair, and we both drift away as the candles burn out and the music stops playing.

CHAPTER 15

BRADLEY

A week has passed by, and my life couldn't get any better than it is now. I have a beautiful fiancé and an adorable daughter. I love them dearly and will work the rest of my life making sure they're happy and well taken care of.

We haven't seen or heard from Tyra, so I'm guessing she's trying to lay low for now, but I'll be ready for her when she shows her evil head. Until then, I will enjoy my life with the woman I want in my bed until the end of time. Our sex life has morphed into something incredible. It's hard to explain. It's like our souls clashing in the never-ending bliss of yearning.

I pull up to the office and get out of the car. Walking through the front door as a new man. "Hey, Mrs. Megan. I hope you enjoyed your weekend."

"Yes, sir, I did. I hear congratulations are in order."

"Yes, thank you."

"I'm so happy for you and Mr. Ryan. So much love in the air."

"That it is."

"Congratulations for what?" Claire asked, coming from the back of the office, holding files in her arms.

"Mr. Bradley here just got engaged to a wonderful soul. I couldn't be happier for the two of you and Mr. Ryan on his marriage and son. I know he's over the moon."

With disappointment in her voice, "Oh, I didn't know. Congratulations," Claire slumberly spits out.

"Thank you, Claire." She rolls her eyes, not realizing I was watching her.

"Is there something wrong, or would like to say, Claire?"

"Oh, no. I have something in my eye. Just trying to get it out."

"Right." I turn to Mrs. Megan. "I will be in my office. I have a couple of accounts to take care of, and then I'm going to take off a little early."

"Yes, Mr. Bradley. If you need anything, I'll be right here."

"Oh right, can you get Mr. Ryan's lawyers on the phone? I would like to set up a meeting with them about some personal matters. Ryan said they are the best in town."

"Sure thing." I then turn and head for my office.

I enter my office and find that the files on my desk have been moved. It probably means nothing. Mrs. Megan and Claire come and go in my office all the time; they probably moved some of them. I just don't really trust Claire just yet. She's a little off for my liking.

I hear my phone ping with a message.

Tyra: *I have your sweet precious, tweety bird. If you want to see her alive again, you will give me my daughter back.*

Dread fills my bones, and fear takes over my mind and soul. I feel myself trembling and my vision blurring. I can't stop my hands from shaking, so I embrace them in the pit of my stomach. "How—

where…" are all the words I can muster up. I pick up my cell and call Amelia.

"Baby, please answer the phone. Please."

"Hi, this is Amelia. Unfortunately, I can't come to the phone…."

I hang up. "Fuck. Think Brad, think."

"Ah, yes. Jason!"

I dial his number, and he answers on the first ring.

"Jason, this is Brad."

"Oh, hey Brad. What's up?"

"She took her. Fuck, that bitch took her."

I get up and run out of the office.

"Slow down, Brad, who took who?"

"Tyra has Amelia. She sent me a text saying that I will give up my daughter if I wanted to see her again. Fuck, what do I do? I don't know what to do?"

"She will be okay. Calm down."

"No, I can't calm the fuck down! That crazy bitch got her, and I need to find her now."

"Amelia has a tracking device installed in her bracelet she wears all the time. I gave it to her last year when her sister went missing. I will bring the app up and find her location. In the meantime, stay at the office; I will be there as soon as possible. Where is Annabelle right now?"

"Shit, she's with the babysitters at Amelia's loft."

"Perfect, tell the babysitter there's a safe room installed in the dance studio. I will text you the password. Tell her to go inside there until one of us comes to get them. She will have everything she needs in that room."

"How—"

"I will explain later. I need you to do this now, Brad. Okay?"

"Got it." He then hangs up the phone.

"Mr. Bradley, is everything okay?" Mrs. Megan ask with concern in her voice.

"No, Amelia is missing. My ex found us, and now she's threatening to kill her if I don't give her Annabelle."

"Oh, no. What can I do?" Mrs. Megan offers.

"Nothing for now. I already called Jason."

I see Claire cowering in the corner like she's been caught doing something.

I call Daphne. She picks up after two rings.

"Daphne, thank God you answered. Is Annabelle with you?"

God, please say yes. Please. "Yes, I just gave her a bath. What's wrong, Mr. Bradley?"

Thank God. "Listen to me. There's a safe room in the dance studio of the loft. Go inside there and take Annabelle with you. It will have everything you need. Then lock yourself inside until I come to get you out. Do you understand?"

"Yes, but what's going on?"

"You remember that woman you saw in the park?"

"Yes."

"She's Annabelle's mother. She tried to kill her once, and she's back to try again. I need you and Annabelle to go inside now. I will text you the password in a second."

"Okay, I'm headed there now."

"Thank you, Daphne."

"Of course, Mr. Bradley. I will take care of her."

I text her the password to the safe room.

"Brad?" Claire calls in a whisper while I send the text to Daphne.

"Yeah?"

"Were you serious about your ex?"

"Yes, why? Why would I lie about that?" I spit out, staring at my phone, waiting for any signs of Amelia being okay.

"Well?"

"Well, what?" I snap, looking at her, and I see her trembling with fear. "Do you know something?"

She pauses for a minute. "Claire, so help me, God, if you don't tell me what the fuck is going on, I will fucking lose my shit. This is my family we're talking about. If you know something, say it now!"

"Brad, I'm sorry. I'm the one who told your ex where you are and where your girlfriend—"

"Fiancé," I corrected her through clinched teeth.

"Sorry, your fiancé. I told her where to find you both. I was upset that you didn't choose me, so when I saw her at the park a couple of weeks ago, I—I…"

"Fucking say it, Claire," I seethed through clenched teeth.

"I gave her your address and where your girl—fiancé, works. She wanted to know her address, but I didn't know it."

"You bitch!" slamming my fist into the wall where she's standing. She physically tenses and starts crying. Mrs. Megan walks around the desk and grabs me by the arm.

"Mr. Bradley, it will be okay. I called the police. They're on their way now," I stare at Claire with such heart wrenching disdain.

I start pacing the room when I get another text, blood dripping from my knuckles. But I don't give two fucks right now.

Tyra: *Don't make me wait too long.*

Me: *Where are you?*

Tyra: *Oh, so you do answer your phone.*

Me: *Stop with the games. Where are you?*

Tyra: *I will tell you where your precious bird is when I see my daughter.*

Me: *How the fuck can I bring her to you if you don't tell me where you are?*

Tyra: *Come home, sweetie, and that's where you will find me.*

Home? Home?

"Right, she's at my house. She won't know if I have Annabelle or not. I have to go."

"Wait, Mr. Bradley, you should wait for the police," Mrs. Megan encourages.

"I can't sit around and do nothing. Besides, I am the police." They both gasp in surprise at my confession. "I'll explain everything later. Right now, I need to find my baby."

I then walk out and call Jason.

"Where is she?"

CHAPTER 16

AMELIA

I flutter my eyes open, and everything is so blurry. My body feels like it has led in it when I try to get up. Finally, I force my eyes to focus, and find I'm in a bedroom or something. The back of my head hurts and throbbing with pain. I feel so groggy, like someone drugged me or something.

"What happened to me? Where am I?"

I try to remember what happened when it all starts flooding back to me. I was walking towards the shop when I heard something behind me. I turned around and saw a dark-skinned woman standing behind me. It's the type of dark that is eerily pleasant on the eyes. Her skin is smooth like dark chocolate savored for this very moment. Yet, her eyes are starkly black, and it frightens me for just a moment. I asked her if everything was okay, and she said, "You have what I want." And then everything went black. I don't remember anything after that.

"Did she hit me with something?" I steady myself and try to open the door. "Shit, it's locked. Of course, it is. I've been kidnapped by god knows who. Why would they leave the door open?" Duh Amelia.

I start searching around the room for a weapon or something useful. I then see the window on the opposite wall and run straight for it.

Only two floors, I can jump and be fine, right? I then try to lift the window. It won't budge. I look down and find the window has been nailed shut. "Shit."

"You won't be leaving that way, so just forget it." I spin around and come face to face with the same woman who looked lost, my abducter.

"What do you want? Who are you?"

"I want my baby and my husband back."

"Your husband?"

"Yes, he was supposed to be married to me until you stole him."

"Tyra?"

"Finally, damn, Brad sure knows how to pick'em."

"I've done nothing to you. Why are you after me?"

"Because you're the bitch trying to play mommy with my baby girl. She's mine and not yours. And now you fucking her daddy like you own him. That's my dick, not yours, and you will never forget that," she seethes through clenched teeth.

"You can't keep me here."

"Yes, I can, and I will."

She slams the door shut and locks it. I start searching for something to protect myself with, and then I realize I can take the hinges off the door. I just need something to push the pin up. I find a hanger in the closet and bend it to be strong enough to force the pin up.

I put my ear up to the door to see if I can hear anything. The coast is clear. I then start wedging the tip of the hanger from the bottom and pushing with all my strength. The first pin pops out.

"Yes! Now for the other two." I continue to do the same with the other two and release the door from the frame. I pry my fingers in between the door and the structure and pulled as hard as possible. I hear the door cracking, and it finally releases completely.

"I'm free! Now, I need to find a phone to call Bradley and pray to God that Annabelle is safe and sound."

I tiptoe along the wall, trying my best not to make a sound. But, unfortunately, I hear crying in the distance, and I know exactly who that is.

"Oh my God! Annabelle."

CHAPTER 17

BRADLEY

"She's in the area of Whittaker Street and Gaston Street near Forsyth Park."

"I know. That's where my rental is. I'm headed there now."

"I know I can't stop you from going to get Amelia back, and I know you're law enforcement but be careful. I'm about twenty minutes out, so you're definitely closure than I am. I also have units headed in that direction as well. Be careful, man, and get my sister the hell out of there."

"I will. I can't lose her. Not now. She means everything to me."

"I know she does. That's why I know I can't stop you. If it was Lily, I would do the same thing. She will be fine. She's a tough girl. Lily taught her well."

"I sure hope so." I then hang up the phone and see that Daphne texted me.

Daphne: *We're okay. I will not leave until I see you or the police coming through that door.*

Me: *Okay, I will be to you soon.*

Daphne: *Okay.*

I'm doing about a hundred miles per hour when I know I should be going slower on these historic streets. I make it to my old house in record time and don't even bother parking the car in a parking space behind the house. I take the stairs two at a time and kick in the door.

"Where the fuck are you, Tyra?"

"Now, is that any way to speak to your wife?" Tyra taunts. "A husband should treat his wife like a queen. Not some whore on the fucking streets," she seethes.

"What the fuck are you talking about?"

"I'm talking about how you left me stranded with nothing. You took everything from me and left. How could you do that to me?" Tyra crying historically.

"You tried to drown our daughter in the bathtub. What did you think was going to happen?"

"Shut up, no, I didn't." She pulls out a gun and points it at me. I raise my hands, surrendering to her. She continues crying and talking crazy. "She wouldn't stop crying. I tried everything. I gave her a bottle, but she wouldn't take it. I changed her diaper, and she really didn't need it. They told me to do it. I tried singing that stupid song you sing to her, but she screamed louder. So, all I wanted to do was shut her up so I could sleep. They told me to do it. I just wanted to sleep for a while, and nothing would work. She loved you more than me, and I hated her for that. I hated you for that, so I want you to suffer just like I did. I want you to feel how I felt when I had nothing," she barks.

I look into Tyra's eyes, and I no longer see the woman I fell in love with all those years ago. I see emptiness. I see rage and hateful resentment surrounding her broken heart. She used to be so loving and caring. She would give you her last and go to find more just to make sure you were okay. I never had that exploding fire in the pit of my stomach the way I have with Amelia, but I still loved the way she was with people. The day we found out she was pregnant was the day she left this earth, and this other person slithered through the night and entered her soul, replacing the kind, loving person with this heartless bitch.

Brad, she's no longer the person who was your best friend. She's no longer the mother of your child. She's no longer the kind and gentle creature. She's the devil's spawn, and you must keep your family safe at all costs. I reach behind my back to retrieve my gun.

"I will see you in hell, my dear husband," she then lifts up the gun and shoots. I feel a sharp pain in my chest, and I look down. My weapon falls out of my hand, dropping to my knees, I place my hands over the pain, and I feel wet warm liquid gliding between my fingers. I look down at my hands, seeing dark, red blood. Again, I fall down, and the next thing I see is Amelia running to my side, my guardian angel, and I drift to sleep feeling no pain, only warmth that the love of my life is lying next to me.

CHAPTER 18

AMELIA

I see Tyra raise the gun, and I run down the hall and push as hard as possible. The gun goes off, and Bradley falls to the floor. I grab the gun from Tyra's hand and throw it across the room. I then rush to Bradley's side.

"Please, God, no. Please be okay, baby. Please be okay. I run into the kitchen to find a cloth to pressure the wound. I then grab a phone and dial 9-1-1.

"911 operator, what is your emergency?"

"My fiancé has been shot in the chest. He has a pulse but a very faint one. I don't have a tourniquet, but I'm putting pressure on the wound. The address is 598 Whittaker Street. My name is Amelia Matthews."

"Ma'am, we already have police headed to that location per Detective Hall. They should be there any minute now."

I then hear movement behind me, so I grab Bradley's gun, turn around and point the gun at Tyra. She comes rushing at me with a knife.

"You bitch. I. HATE. YOU," she screams, charging at me, preparing to stab me. I pull the trigger twice, hitting her in the chest. She continues after me, so I pull the trigger two more times, hitting her in the head this time. Finally, she drops to the floor, blood oozing from her head, mouth, and chest.

"Who's the bitch now!"

"Ma'am, Ma'am? Are you okay?"

I pick up the phone. "Yes, I'm okay. I just shot my fiancé's ex. Please hurry; he needs an ambulance now.

A few seconds later, Jason comes running through the door with three other officers.

"Jason, please help him. He's been shot. He's still breathing, but he has a weak pulse. He needs to get to the hospital now."

"We got it from here, Amelia. Are you okay?"

"Yes, I'm fine. She drugged me with something and hit me with something, but other than that, I'm good. But, oh my gosh, where's Annabelle? I heard crying in one of the other rooms before I tried to stop her from shooting Bradley."

"Amelia, Annabelle is safe. She's with the babysitter. I sent Lily there to pick her up."

"Oh my gosh, thank God," wrapping my arms around him. Jason is always here, saving me. I finally pull away, "I want to go with him to the hospital. I can help."

"Okay, I will be right behind you."

"And what about her?"

"Oh, she's dead. Two in the chest and two in the head. Just like you taught me."

I then rush out of the house right beside Bradley, my future husband. He will make it through this. We both will.

CHAPTER 19

BRADLEY

*B*eep. Beep. Beep. The only sound I hear.

Beep. Beep. Beep. Where is that coming from?

Beep. Beep. Beep. It's dark all around. I can't see anything.

I can't talk; trying to open my mouth and speak is beyond impossible.

I can't hear anything else; my ears are closed to all other sounds.

I feel numb all over my body. I can't move. My legs feel like cement drying in the sun; my arms are like Jell-O on a cool summer morning.

What the fuck is going on?

Then a bright light flashes in my eyes, and I feel so calm, like drifting waters surrounding me or rain sprinkling on my face, washing over me.

I hear crying in the distance, and I know that cry. Who is that?

I have a strong feeling I know that voice, but the light. I have a strong desire to drift towards the light, but the crying and the beeping. I need to find out who's crying.

"It's okay, baby girl. Daddy will be okay." Who is that? I know that voice. I need to find out who that is.

The light is so soothing and pure. I turn for the light.

"Da, da!"

"Da, da!"

CHAPTER 20

AMELIA

*I*t's easy to describe unbearable fear when faced with danger like a gun pointed at your head, and the only thing you see is the long deep hallow tunnel of the barrel. Everything is moving at a slow pace, and the sight of lent flowing in the air at the speed rate of a snail is the only thing that keeps you focused or calm.

But the fear I have now is unspeakable. It's an overwhelming feeling I can't pass on to the next person. This is the fear I have to face alone, and no one can take that away.

We're laughing, and it's been a perfect day, my sixteenth birthday has finally come, and I'm finally becoming a woman. We have always gone out to dinner for my birthday, and this day will be no different. Well, except for Lily not being here. I so miss my big sister. But she off pursuing her dreams, becoming a nurse just like our mother.

We're on the highway, heading to the downtown area when we see bright lights in our lane. They're so blinding, and they hurt.

"Mommy, Daddy," I scream.

"Baby, it's okay. Put your head down now."

"*Will, move; they're going to hit us,*" my mom screams out.

I feel the car jerk very hard and swerve into the opposite lane. I then feel an incredible pain shooting through my legs and back. My head flies forward, and my body jerks back. I hear glass shattering and my mother screaming for dear life. The movement comes to a halt, and the screaming has stopped. My head hurts so much, but it's nothing like the pain in my legs. I can't move.

"*Mom? Dad?*" *I say through the silence in the car, my voice cutting through the air.*

"*Mom, can you hear me?*" *once again, sickening silence.*

"*We have to get out of the car. Please, daddy, wake up,*" *I cry out. More silence. I try to move, but it hurts so much. I unbuckle my seatbelt and slide on my side in the backseat. I think my legs are broken, and my right arm is broken. I'm in excruciating pain, and I'm about to pass out. But I can't. Not now. I have to get us out of here.*

I feel for my phone in my pocket and dial 9-1-1.

"*911 operator, what is your emergency?*"

"*There was a car accident, and my parents are hurt.*"

"*Are you okay? Where are you?*"

"*I think my legs are broken, but I'm okay. We're on Highway 80, heading into Savannah from Wilmington Island. A car came into our lane, and my dad swerved to avoid hitting them, but they hit us anyway.*"

"*Can you get out of the car?*"

"*I'm trying now, but I can't leave my parents.*"

"*We have help on the way. I need you to get out of the car if you can. What is your name?*"

"*My name is Amelia Matthews. My parents are Yulanda and William Matthews.*"

"*Okay, you're doing good.*"

"*My head hurts, and I want to go to sleep.*"

"No, you must stay awake, Amelia. I have units on their way to you now."

"I hear the sirens. They're coming. I need to close my eyes," I whisper in the phone.

"No, don't close your eyes. Can you see the other car?"

"No."

"Okay. You're doing good."

"I'm out of the car, but I can't move anymore. I'm so tired."

"Amelia, are you still with me?"

"Amelia?" I feel someone shaking my shoulders.

"Amelia?"

"Yes, huh?" I say to whoever is shaking me. "I'm up."

"Are you okay? You were talking in your sleep. Something about your mom and dad."

"Yes, I'm okay. How is he? How's Bradley?" I ask the doctor gaining an understanding of where I am and deflecting the doctor's questions.

I'm right back at the hospital. I've been here so many times I've lost track of how many times.

"He's not out of woods yet. We've already completed three surgeries, and it was a little touchy, but for now, he's doing okay. We will know more when he wakes up, and we complete the last surgery."

"What all did you have to do?" I ask the doctor.

"Well, the bullet nipped his heart and ruptured the main artery. He's fortunate to be alive. He probably would have bled to death if you didn't put pressure on his wound. You saved him, not us."

I put my head in my hands, and I just start crying. I'm crying for Bradley, I'm crying for Annabelle, I'm crying for my parents, I'm crying for everything that has ever happened to this family.

"It's okay, Amelia. Let it out. This is a lot to handle. Do you have support at home?" The doctor is rubbing my back, trying to soothe me during my apparent meltdown.

"Yes, I have support. I just… I just can't right now."

"I understand. We're about to start his last surgery. I think you should call some family members to sit with you. I know you're not going home anytime soon."

"They're on their way. My sister is picking up Annabelle now. I want her close to me."

"That's a good idea."

"What's your name? I'm sorry. You might have told me, but I've been in and out."

"I understand. Dr. Stacy Storm."

"Thank you, Dr. Storm. I appreciate everything."

"You're welcome dear."

CHAPTER 21

BRADLEY

*"A*nnabelle, who's daddy's baby girl?"

"Da, da."

"Yes, baby girl. Daddy."

"Ma, ma."

"Where's mommy?" Annabelle points to a woman, and I turn around. She's the most beautiful woman I've ever seen. The sun surrounding her like the angel she is. Her hair gliding through the wind like waves splashing on a beach. Her skin is as smooth as a milky way, and those eyes, my god. Her eyes can capture the hearts of the world and break many souls.

"Yes, baby girl. That's your mommy."

It's a beautiful day at the beach, and Amelia, Annabelle, and I are having a picnic on the sand outside of our beach house. Amelia made finger sandwiches for all of us, and she's holding Lila Marie in her arms. Together we made a beautiful baby girl with Amelia's eyes and hair and my stubbornness.

Both of our girls are heartbreakers. I feel sorry for the poor saps that will try to break their hearts. I have something coming to them if they do.

I look into the eyes of Amelia, and she smiles at me with those perfect teeth shining. I then feel a sharp pain in my chest, and I grab my heart. I look down at my hands, and they're stained with blood. I look into Amelia's eyes again, and I see pure fear and rage in her gentle gaze. I reach out to her, but I can't seem to feel her.

"What's happening? Why does it hurt so much?"

Everything is turning grey, and I can no longer see my girls. Where are my girls? I need my girls!

I feel a strong shock in my chest. "Ouch, that hurts!"

CHAPTER 22

AMELIA

*I*t's been nine days, and Bradley still has not woken up. So I've been here for almost two weeks, and I haven't moved yet. And I'm not going to move until the love of my life wakes up.

I feel strength being by his side. I know he will wake up soon. I know he will. I just know it.

Lily has been a godsend. She has taken care of Annabelle and the triplets while I stay by my fiancé's side. She and Jason, Kim and Ryan, and Dianella have all taken turns coming to sit with me. They are the best family a person can ask for, but I really just want my love back.

I want his strength back. I need his love back, his comfort back. He can't leave me now. We've just begun our life together.

"Please, Bradley. Please come back to me," I sob softly to myself.

The nurse walks in to take his vitals.

"How is Mr. Bradley doing today?"

"Well, his blood pressure is normal, and his heartbeat is stronger than ever. So I think he's having a better day than yesterday," I reply. My voice sounding so foreign to me.

"That he is. If you need anything, please let me know. We're here for you, Amelia."

"Thank you, Erica."

"Of course, we nurses have to stick together," she then smiles at me, a genuine smile, and then walks out.

It's just me, Bradley, and the multiple sounds alarming around the room. The nurse was nice enough to roll another bed in here for me to lay on because they knew I wasn't leaving his side until he woke up.

I don't care what anyone says; I'm not leaving him. He's my heart and soul. I have faith that he will wake up soon.

CHAPTER 23

BRADLEY

"*D*a, da."

I hear my baby girl, but I don't see her. She's calling me daddy for the first time. I want to see my baby girl again.

Let me see my baby girl!

"Oh my gosh. Yes, sweetie. That's daddy," I hear Amelia say. I listen to her crying as she encourages Annabelle to call for me again.

"Da, da."

"Yes, sweetie. Daddy will be okay. He's just sleeping. We have to wait for him to wake up," says Amelia. I try so hard to call out to her. But she doesn't hear me.

"Amelia?" I announce, not sure if she heard me.

"Oh my God! Bradley? Baby, are you awake?" I feel her grab my hand and squeeze. Everything is so groggy.

My mouth is dry, like cotton. I cough because my throat hurts, and it's so dry.

"Here, take a sip of water slowly." She put the straw in my mouth, and I take a sip of water like Amelia tells me. The ice-cold water is soothing and refreshing; I take another sip and then another.

"Babe, not so much. You haven't eaten in weeks. You will make yourself throw up if you drink too much."

I cough because my throat still hurts a little. "Where am I? How long have I've been here?" I sound so terrible.

"Well, it's been a little over three months since you came to the hospital. Do you remember anything?"

"Three months?" I ask, astounded.

"Yes. It was a little hairy for a minute there, but you're a strong guy. I push the button to call for Dr. Storm. She can give a better update than I can."

"Baby, how are you holding up?" She looks surprised that I even ask. I can see the bags under her eyes, black rings circling them. She's loss weight and worrisome etched on her beautiful face.

"I'm okay. I'm more worried about you. I...I...I can't."

The doctor walks in right when she was about to say something.

"Hi, Mr. Philips. I'm Dr. Stacy Storm. How are you feeling today?"

"I'm good, just a little stiff. The drugs must be good because I don't feel any pain."

Laughing, "Well, yes. You are on some pain blockers for now. I would like you to stay overnight just so we can monitor you a little more. Do you remember anything that happened the night you came in?"

"Not really. I remember Amelia standing over me, and that's about it," squeezing her hand to let her know she and Annabelle are the reason I'm here today. "I don't remember coming here at all."

"Yeah, I was about to tell him what happened when you came in, Dr. Storm."

163

"Okay, Amelia. It's good that I'm here just in case."

"Just in case? What's going on? I glance between the both of them. Both the doctor and Amelia look at each other before Amelia speaks. I can see the hesitation in Amelia's demeanor, and it's scaring the fuck out of me.

"Well, your ex, Tyra, decided to kidnap me from the café. She drugged me and then took me to your house and locked me in one of the rooms. When I figured out a way to get out, I heard you and her arguing downstairs, so I hurried to you. But I was too late." She drops her head into her hands and starts rocking back and forth.

"It's okay, Amelia. You did what you could," I encourage her.

"That's not all of it. After she shot you, I pushed her to the ground, causing her to drop her gun, and I thought I knocked her out, but when I tried to stop the bleeding, I heard her coming up behind me and she had a knife in her hand," pausing for what seemed forever, I encouraged her to continue. "She was trying to kill me too, so I did the only thing I could. I grabbed your gun, and I shot her twice, but she kept coming like it didn't even phase her; killing her was my only option. I had no choice. I am so sorry, Bradley. I didn't want to hurt her, but I had no choice," tears rolling down her face, and she's still the most beautiful angel I've ever seen. My guardian angel.

Clearing my throat, "Amelia, sweetie. It's okay. I understand. Tyra was out of her mind when she killed my mother. You did what you had to do to protect yourself, me, and Annabelle. I do not fault you for that. And I'm not mad at you for doing what's right by our family. Do you understand, Amelia? I love you, and I know you will always protect Annabelle and me if we need you."

"I know, but it was her mother. I took her mother from her. You might forgive me, but she never will. How do we tell her that her mother is dead, and I'm why she died."

"Amelia, we will cross that bridge when we get there. She's only, shit. How long have I been in here again?"

"A little over three months, why?"

"What day is it?" I ask.

"October fourth."

"Shit, Annabelle's first birthday. It was October first. I missed my daughter's birthday."

"Oh. My. Gosh. I didn't realize it. I was so caught up with you and everything. Shoot. I can't believe this. How in the world did I forget Annabelle's birthday?"

"Amelia, you had so much going on. I'm not surprised you didn't forget more than just that," Dr. Storm says to Amelia.

"Yes, Amelia. The Doc is right. We will get through this together. Besides, she won't know the difference; she can't even talk yet."

"Um, well. I beg to differ. She's saying Daddy and Mommy now. Well, da, da and ma, ma."

"Holy, shit! I did hear her voice."

"What do you mean?" Dr. Storm inquires.

"I thought I was dreaming that Annabelle was calling me, and then she said Ma, ma and pointed to Amelia. It felt so real, and I can't believe I remember that."

"Dreams sometimes depict the reality of our lives. You want a life with Amelia, and you want your daughter to accept Amelia as a motherly figure in her life. There is nothing wrong with that, and actually, it's a healthy depiction of your future with Amelia and Annabelle. You crave a family, and you have one. Right here," she points to Amelia and Annabelle.

"Dr. Storm, I get what you are saying, but how do I replace her mother? I never wanted that, and it's not fair to Annabelle," Amelia cries out in defeat.

"Amelia, you can never replace her mother, but you can raise her as your own. Give her love and guidance that her mother cannot give to her. Show her that you love her, care for her, and never leave her side. She needs your love and support. She will crave it, and she will see you as her mother whether you want it or not. She's too young to remember her mother. You can tell her about her mother when she gets old enough, but you are her mother right now," Dr. Storm explains.

I know Amelia is having a hard time with this, and she has every right to feel some type of way, but I need her to know that I support her in every way. She needs to know that I will not leave her hanging or force her to do anything she doesn't want to do. But why can't the words come out when I need them to? Why? She needs to hear you say the words. Open your fucking mouth.

"Amelia?"

"Yes?" She looks so defeated. I sit up in the bed and feel a sharp pain in my chest.

"Please be careful, Bradley. I need you to take it easy," Amelia demands while assisting me in sitting up.

"I will. I just need you to understand one thing."

"I'm listening."

"You are the love of my life. I know this more now than I ever have before. I have not changed my mind about marrying you. I want you to be a mother to my child, all my children. I want you to know that I support you to the bitter end. I am not leaving you, and I have no desire to put anyone else before you. You will be my wife, sooner than later, and you will be the mother of my child, sooner than later. I've already started the process before all of this shit started; I just wanted it to be a surprise, but I needed to say this now and not later. I love you, Amelia and Annabelle loves you. You are the only person I want in my life and Annabelle's life. Please, baby, I need you."

Tears are flowing down her cheeks like tiny streams of water flowing down a riverbank. Her eyes are red and blotchy, and even now, she still looks radiantly beautiful to me. This woman risked her life to save mine, and I will spend the rest of my life giving her everything she deserves and more. Her unspoken words only solidify our strength and companionship. She doesn't have to say a word. I know what's in her heart.

She stands up and bends over my bed and kisses me softly on my lips. My god, her lips feel like blankets of clouds, and her tongue enters my taste buds exploding with rainbow skittles bursting with each swipe. Three months I've missed these delectable lips on mine, and I shall have them again.

The machines start beeping loudly because my heart rate has increased.

"Okay, okay, we can't have your heart rate increasing just yet. You literally just came out of a coma," Dr. Storm explains with humor in her tone.

Amelia pulls away with a loud smack, taking a deep breath, evident that she did not want to stop. I, too, feel lost without her lips on mine.

"Okay, Doc. I will follow your orders, but I can't promise that it will last long," we all laugh. "Ugh, that hurts," I complain.

"It will hurt for a while in your chest area and ribs. Getting plenty of rest and no physical exertion will help with the healing."

"I will make sure he follows the rules, Dr. Storm. We just hired a new manager at the café to help Dianella, so I will be home through his entire recovery."

"That's good to hear."

Annabelle started to wake up, so the Doc excused herself so we could talk as a family.

"Good afternoon, Sunshine. How's my favorite girl?" Amelia says. She picks her up to bring her to my bed. "Say hi, daddy. Can you say hi, daddy?"

"Da, da," Annabelle coos. Tears wailing up in my eyes and I feel overwhelming happiness to be here with my baby girl.

"Yes, sweetheart. Daddy is here. I'm right here." Amelia places her in my lap, and I try to wrap my arms around her. I feel pain, but I don't care. I live for this moment just to have my girls in my arms.

Annabelle wraps her little arms around my neck and squeezes a little. "Da, da," she then starts blowing spit bubbles with her lips.

"She just started that habit. I can't bear to tell her to stop. She's so cute when she does it," Amelia smiles.

"Yes, she does with those cute little cheeks. But, unfortunately, her eyes are becoming greyer like mine as well. I feel like I've missed so much while I was out."

"No, you haven't missed much. We've been here every day. Lily and Dianella had to bring me clothes, make me eat, and take showers because I didn't want to miss the moment you woke up. I wanted our faces to be the first face you saw when you opened your eyes."

"So, you're not working?" I probe her.

"No, I couldn't leave your side, and Dianella, Lily, and Jason under-stood. We were able to hire a nice girl to help out at the café. I will return once you're doing better."

"I understand; I just don't want to stop you from doing what you love."

"I love being right here by your side. This is where I belong."

"Thank you, Amelia. Thank you for everything."

"No need to thank me. I'm your protector. No more being bounded by fear."

"That you are."

With Annabelle in her arms, she leans over and gives me another kiss. Not as long as before, but it's worth every second she provides.

CHAPTER 24

AMELIA

"*Annabelle, sweetie. I hear you. Where are you, my sweet girl?*"

"*Where the fuck are you, Tyra?*" *I hear Bradley yell. Thank god, he's here to save us.*

"*Now, is that any way to speak to your wife?*" *she taunts.* "*A husband should treat his wife like a queen. Not some whore on the fucking streets.*"

"*What the fuck are you talking about?*" *he asks.*

"*I'm talking about how you left me stranded with nothing. You took everything from me and left. How could you do that to me?*" *she cries out.*

"*You tried to drown our daughter in the bathtub. What did you think was going to happen?*"

The crying stops, so I decided to walk down the stairs to help Bradley. Annabelle will be okay for just a moment. Once I make it downstairs, I see Tyra holding a gun up and aimed at Bradley.

"*Shut up, no, I didn't,*" *she starts crying hysterically and talking crazy. Her back is facing me, so I slowly walk up behind her.* "*She wouldn't stop crying. I tried everything. I gave her a bottle, but she wouldn't take it. They told me to do it. I changed her diaper, and she really didn't need it. I tried singing that stupid song you sing to her, but she screamed louder. They told me to do it! So, all I wanted to do was shut her up so I could sleep. I just wanted to sleep for a while, and nothing would work. She loved you more than she loved me, and I hated her for that. I hated you for that, so I want you to suffer just like I did. I want you to feel how I felt when I had nothing," Tyra threatens through gapping screams.*

"I will see you in hell, my dear husband.""I then rush up behind her and push her as hard as possible. The gun goes off, she drops to the floor, hitting her head on the coffee table. The gun falls out of her hand, and she sits there lifeless.

I run over to Bradley, "Please, god no. Please be okay, baby. Please be okay." I run into the kitchen to find a cloth to pressure the wound. I then grab a phone and dial 9-1-1.

"911 operator, what is your emergency?"

"My fiancé has been shot in the chest. He has a pulse but a very faint one. I don't have a tourniquet, but I'm putting pressure on the wound. The address is 598 Whittaker Street. My name is Amelia Matthews."

"Ma'am, we already have police headed to that location per Detective Hall. They should be there any minute now."

I then hear movement behind me, so I grab Bradley's gun, turn around and point the gun at Tyra. But, instead, she comes rushing at me with a knife.

"You bitch! I. HATE. YOU," she screams, preparing to stab me. I pull the trigger twice, hitting her in the chest. She continues after me, so I shoot two more times in the head this time. She drops to the floor, blood oozing from her head, mouth, and chest.

"No, No, No! Please god, no," I scream.

"Amelia, baby. Please wake up," Bradley calls out.

"Amelia!" Bradley yelling at me. He's shaking me, trying to wake me up.

"Huh, stop. Get off me," I scream, scooting to the edge of the bed.

"Amelia, it's me, Bradley."

"Bradley?" I inquire.

"Yes, it's Bradley. You were having a nightmare. You were calling for me. Are you okay?"

I sit up in bed, drenched in sweat. The dream felt so real because it was real. It did happen, and I keep reliving that horrific day over and over when I close my eyes.

"Yes, I'm okay," gasping for air.

"Do you want to talk about it?"

"Not really." I can't talk about this, not this. It's all my fault.

"Okay, but do know, I'm here. I'm okay. You're okay. Annabelle is okay. You can talk to me about anything."

"I know. I just—I." I place my head in my hands, and I start crying. I hate crying, but lately, I've cried more than I ever have.

Bradley wraps his arms around my shoulders and flinches in obvious pain, but he tries to comfort me anyway. I don't argue. I don't push him away because, in this moment, I need him. I need him to take away the nightmares. I need him to protect me from the evils. I almost lost him four months ago, and that pain was just like the pain I felt when I lost my parents. It might have been worse, knowing that I could do nothing to save him or help him. I should have done more. I could have done more. It's all my fault.

"Baby, look at me." I ignore him because I don't want him to see me like this, like this weak little girl.

"Please, look at me," he begs. He places his hand under my chin and lifts it up so I can look into his eyes. My gosh, those eyes are so mesmerizing and calming, I instantly feel an overflowing of warmth rush over my body and into my heart, soothing me. "Do you know when I was a little boy, I used to have nightmares?" He asks rhetorically. "My mother used to come into my room, wrap her arms around me, and just hold me. She would rock me back and forth in her arms to calm me down and soothe me the best way she knew how. You see, my mother was trying to protect me from the nightmares I was having because she knew I saw my father beating her on many occasions, but she never said anything about it. She just held me and rocked me back and forth. To think about it, I had forgotten all about the nightmares until now. I think I pushed those memories far away, and I honestly don't know why."

"I know why. Your father beating your mother was so traumatic; your body or brain suppressed the memories to help you cope. Your suppressed memories are coming back now because you are finally ready to deal with them. They are not there to hurt you or ruin the life you have created for yourself. Instead, the memories are coming back to help you make sense of why things are the way they are, that it's time to work through them and that you are safe enough to do so."

"Wow, when you put it that way, it makes a whole lot of sense. I just wish it would have come back a lot sooner. I have so many questions for my mom. I want to know if he's still alive and if he is, where is he? But this is not about me right now. This is about you. Amelia, you're suffering, and I don't want you to suffer anymore."

"I think this is about us. So much has happened in the last several months that we haven't had the chance of a normal life. We've faced death several times in our lives, and for what? Because we want the American dream or just want peace or just maybe we want this trauma to go away; that every time there's happiness, there's pain to follow, like unbearable pain, unforgiving fear."

"I don't think it's like that. God wouldn't put anything on us that we couldn't handle. I believe you told me that." He flashes that perfect smile at me, and I begin to melt all over again. "There's a reason we're going through this, and I think we were chosen to go through it together. I would have never met you if it wasn't for Ryan and Kim taking a day to shop at St. John's Town Center. That was pure fate that he blessed me with an opportunity to get myself back on my feet and invite Annabelle and me to his vacation home while you were there. I believe we belong together, and I will continue to fight for us," he professes.

I put my hands on each side of his face, holding his cheeks in my palms. "You do not have to fight for us. You already have me, and I have you. We shall fight together. We have proven two is better than one in any situation." I drop my hands and place them in my lap while we still sit in the bed in the middle of the night. "I was dreaming about that night. I haven't been able to sleep well since that night. Watching you being shot and then me having to shoot and kill your ex was very disturbing for me, not in the sense that it wasn't right, but having to be forced to do it. My sister was forced to kill her kidnappers and rapists just two years ago while being raped. And my best friend had to kill several people, including her own father and her ex, because they too raped and tried to kill her. And now, I did the same, and I'm scared. I'm scared that our love won't be enough."

I get out of bed because I don't want him to try to comfort me right now. I'm mad as hell. I'm insanely furious, not at him, but at the situation we both were put in.

"Amelia, I get it. You're worried if we can't survive this, that our love alone can't survive this. Well, I know that if we stick together, we can survive anything we put our minds to. Look at us now, you were attacked in the streets of Savannah, and if I hadn't been there, there's no telling what would've happened. If you couldn't free yourself from that prison Tyra set up for you, I would not be alive today. I'm convinced that you are my guardian angel. Will there be times when we aren't there together? Absolutely. But that does not mean that we won't find ourselves alone at times praying that the other was there. I may be at work, and something may happen or vice-versa. As long as we are a united front, we shall prevail against all obstacles."

I have my back to him looking out the window, and I hear everything he's saying to me. Of course, I understand everything he's saying to me, and still, I fear I may lose him. "Amelia, look at me?"

I slowly turn around and meet his gaze. "Do you have faith in us?" He asks me.

He is looking at me, and he is waiting for an answer that I'm not sure I can answer. I'm terrified in this moment. I'm hurting in this moment. I don't think I have the strength to answer him, let alone agree with his statements. I should, but I'm not sure I can right now.

"Amelia, please answer the question."

"Bradley, I don't think that I can."

"What do you mean? You don't have faith in us? You don't believe we can overcome the evil that has graced us with its ugly head?" Shaking my head violently because I can't bear to have him upset with me. "If anything, we should be able to trust one another with our lives, souls, and hearts."

Crying once again. Hell, I don't think I'll ever stopped crying; I find myself falling apart. Bradley gets out of bed slowly because he's still in so much pain from the surgery. He wraps his arms around my waist, and I want to break free, but I feel the calming spread over me, once again. He holds me tight in his embrace, and I melt at his touch.

"Amelia, do you feel that? Do you feel the overwhelming calm that we give each other by a single touch? Do you not feel protected by my embrace? Do you not feel safe in my arms? Because if you don't, it's time for me to leave. I will not bring harm to you or anyone else ever again."

I pull forward and turn around to face him. "No, you can't leave! I do feel the overwhelming calming of your embrace. I feel safe in your arms, and I love you with all my heart! I just—I just don't want...."

"You don't want us to end up like your parents or my parents."

The unspoken words I've dreaded to think or say out loud have flooded my ears. My heart begins to race, and I feel light-headed.

Finally, my legs give out, and Bradley, even through his injury, finds the strength to hold me up.

"Baby, I told you. I get it. I understand your fears, but if you don't face your fears head-on, you will miss the best thing that has ever happened to you, to us. I know you're scared, but nothing can hurt or come between us if we catch each other when we fall."

I sit down on the window ledge and pull Bradley down with me. I take his hands into mine, holding them in my lap. I take my ring off every night before I go to bed, and right now, I feel naked without it on.

As I look at my nightstand where my ring rests each night, I remember the promise and devotion that Bradley professed to me only months ago.

"Annabelle and I have been talking, and we decided that we want you a part of our family. We've loved you since the moment we saw you. You're kind-loving, and you are a beautiful soul inside and out. You brighten our lives and have brought warmth into our hearts when we least expected it. You were willing to give us everything when we needed you the most, and we will forever be thankful to have someone like you in our lives. Annabelle and I have been through a lot, and so have you, but we can conquer the world." He bends down on one knee with Annabelle sitting on that knee. He reaches into his pocket and pulls out a small box. I feel tears running down my cheek, and my lips are trembling with joy. "Amelia Matthews, baby, will you do us the honor of being my wife."

How can I let such a wonderful man like Bradley Philips slip through my fingers? He's everything I look for in a man. He actually reminds me of my dad, strong, loving, devoting, and uplifting, not only for himself but for Annabelle and me. He's right, I am lucky to have such a strong, devoted man by my side, and I would be absolutely crazy to let him go. Besides, I love Annabelle probably more than I love him.

"You're right," I announce.

"I am?" he asks, with bewilderment in his tone.

"Yes, I'm terrified of losing you, not because of infidelity, but because of outside factors. My parents were very loving towards me and Lily, and they loved each other. There were times when we would catch them kissing when they thought we weren't looking or my dad smacking my mom on her ass. At the time, we thought it was the grossest thing in the world, but now I understand their passion for one another. I see it with Lily and Jason, and I see it with you and me. I want us to be partners, but I also fear the unknown."

"Amelia, you can't be afraid of what might or what might not happen. You have to have faith that we will survive every obstacle thrown our way, whether it's good or bad."

"I know, and I will certainly try to be more understanding of every circumstance that we encounter.z'

"That's all I'm asking, Amelia; your understanding and devotion to our family."

I wrap my arms around his neck and embrace him in my arms. His head rests on my breast, and I feel the overwhelming calming once again. "Do you feel that?"

"Yes, your overwhelming calming nature has taken over me."

"No, it's your calming nature that takes over my mind, body, and soul."

"How about this? Our mind, body, and soul react to our over-whelming calming nature to bring us closer together."

He then reaches up to kiss me on my lips, and I immediately feel tingling all over my body. Does he feel that too? He pulls away with clouded dreamy eyes.

"Amelia, baby, I need you." I then look down, and he's completely aroused and standing at attention.

"Bradley, we can't. The doctor has not cleared you for sexual activity."

"What if you show him a little attention? I promise I won't rip your clothes off, bend you over the bed, and fuck you into the next century."

"Sure, am I supposed to believe that? You can't help yourself. And besides, I'm afraid your heart rate may cause some problems."

"I'll be having problems if I can't get inside you one way or another."

"Okay, okay, but no intercourse." His face lights up when I finally give in.

"Okay, I promise to be good." I roll my eyes because I know he's full of shit.

While sitting on the edge of the window, he drops his boxers on the floor. He's so eager to feel my lips around his dick. So, I lean forward and take his length into my hands. Then, I wrap my lips around his head, licking the tip with my tongue.

"Fuck, that feels so good, baby."

I then drag my tongue down his shaft, and he visibly shutters. I slowly take his entire length into my mouth, and I suck softly like a lollipop. Just how he showed me before.

"Oh my god, baby…Jesus, I'm about to come."

I slow my ravishing because I want him to enjoy this as long as he can withstand the torture. I then let his dick slip out of my mouth, and I wrap my lips around both of his balls and gently rotate them in my mouth. Next, he sticks his hand in my hair and wraps it around his fist; gently pulling on it, causing me to flinch a little, but I accept the pleasurable pain more than I thought I would.

I then release his balls and put his dick back in my mouth, and I suck, and I suck some more. I want him to feel what I feel when he pleasures me. I want him to forget all the pain he suffered in the past four months. I want him to be immensely devoted to this moment.

"I love this shit, baby. You are really getting good at this. I can't hold on any longer, baby. I'm about to come." I then feel his dick swell even more in my mouth, and I suck through my gag reflex.

"Shit, I'm coming, baby." I feel warm liquid squirt in my mouth and run down my tongue and into my throat, and I drink every bit of his essence he gives me. I marvel in his salty yet sweet cream of pleasure. I continue to suck because I want more. I need more.

"Ooh, baby. Not so hard. It's extremely sensitive. Oh, god. Baby, I'm still coming. Shit."

He continues to empty his load inside my mouth, and it tastes so amazing; I forget that his dick is very sensitive and had to release him a little. However, he still has not grown soft, and I fear he needs more attention.

"Baby, please, I need to feel you," reading the very thoughts that emerge my mind.

"Bradley, we can't. I don't want to hurt you."

"What if you were on top? I won't be doing anything but sitting there. Please, baby, I need you?" he begs.

I gape at his pouting face, and just the gander in his gaze, I have no choice but to give in. I knew he would sucker me into giving him what he wanted.

"Okay fine, but if I see the slightest discomfort, I'm stopping. I don't care how good it feels to either of us."

"Thanks, babe," helping me stand with a bit of pep in his step. It's like four in the morning, and we've been up for hours talking and crying and talking some more.

He scoots on the bed and waits for me to take my nightshirt off. Really, it's his t-shirt, but whatever. It's mine for now. I then take my panties off, and he watches every movement I make, getting aroused all over again. His bandage is across his chest, and even with that on, he looks like a Greek god, returned from battle.

I climb on top of him with my legs straddled on either side of his hips. My pussy is so wet that I feel moisture running down my legs.

"Fuck baby, you are so fucking wet right now. You're driving me crazy."

"I hope not too crazy; I need you to maintain a safe heart rate."

"I need to take care of you like you took care of me." He then lifts up and flips me on my back, diving between my legs. His lips sucking my pussy like it's his last time ever tasting me again.

"Bradley, fuck. You shouldn't—Oh, my god, that feels good. Please, baby, don't stop," completely driving me insane. I have no self control left in me.

He then licks my clit, and I feel myself shutter throughout my body. I know we shouldn't be doing this, but my body has a mind of its own at this point. I want, no, I need him more than I realize.

"Bradley, please. I'm about to—Ah, oh my god, Bradley."

"That's it, baby; I want to feel you; I want to taste you come inside my mouth."

And just like that, I feel an overwhelming desire to give him what he want and need from my body. Screaming on the top of my lungs in the privacy of our home, I release all of my doubts, fears, desires, wants and needs, and soul. I give him everything I have and more.

He drinks from me. He takes from me. He has the power to do whatever he wants to me, and I will give it all to him. I will give this sexy paragon all of me.

He releases my pussy after I come down from my ecstasy high, and he prepares to get on top of me.

"Oh, no, you don't. You might have overpowered me on this one, but you, sir, will lay your ass down now. It's my turn." He then gives me that pouty face, and I don't fall for it this time. "Lay your ass down now," I say again as I get up off the bed to look more authoritative.

He looks at me with obvious shock on his face. "Yes, ma'am."

He then lays on the bed on his back with his hands resting behind his head. Really to get a great view of my perky breast and curvy waist. But I don't care. I want him to look at me like a piece of meat. I'm his forage of choice for the night, morning, or whatever the fuck day it is.

I climb on top of him, and his mouth goes straight for my breast. He puts one taunt nipple in his mouth while he plays with the other one. I try not to put my weight on his chest because I don't want to hurt him or break open the staples. Instead, I use his shoulders for support and guide my body down his shaft while he sucks and pinches my nipples. I feel his dick sink so deep inside of me; I flinch a little at the intrusion. His dick is so notably distinguished and substantial that sometimes I don't even know how he fits inside me.

Once my body adjusts to him, I begin to use his shoulder to help me guide up and down his massive dick.

"Oh my god, I've missed this so much. Bradley, you feel so good." He then pops my nipple out of his mouth, moaning and concentrating on his task at hand.

"You feel amazing, babygirl." I swirl my hips like he does, and holy shit, that right there feels fucking phenomenal . "Fuck, Amelia. That feels fucking sensational." He places his hands on my hips and helps me move up and down his shaft. "That's it, baby. Squeeze that dick. It's all yours."

I rock back and forth as hard as I can, and I feel myself about to come. "That's it, baby, give it to me. I want to feel you come around this dick. That's it. Harder, baby. Give it to me harder." He rubs my clit with his thumb, and I explode, feeling my essence flow out of me and around his dick like caramel being drizzled on chocolate ice cream. I arch my back, and I hold my head back while enjoying the ride of a lifetime. I continue to ride his dick needing to feel him inside me. I've become so weak after my orgasm, he does all the work with his arms for me.

"Bradley, I want to feel you come inside of me. Can you do that for me?"

"Of course, baby, I will give you the world and more if I could. I need you to fuck this dick like no other."

"Okay." I then rock harder and harder on his dick, using the headboard for support. I fuck him so hard; I begin to ache. But I ignore the pain and give him what he wants. I feel my walls gripping him again. "Shit Bradley, I'm about to come again," totally shocked at the multiple orgasms this man can demand from me.

"That's what I want, baby. I want to feel you come with me." I then push harder and harder, and I feel him swell inside of me, and at the same time, we have the best fucking orgasm in the world.

"Shhhhiiiittttt, fuck Amelia. Goddamnit. You feel fucking amazing." I then collapse on his chest, forgetting that he just had surgery.

"Shit, Bradley. I'm sorry."

"It's okay, baby. I'm fine. The stitches are healing perfectly because of you." He pulls me to his chest, and I rest my head on his hard, beastly slab. He runs his fingers through my hair, and I'm still sitting on his dick, feeling both of our cum running out of me and down his ass cheeks. I prepare to clean up, but he pulls me back down. "I don't want you to go anywhere. You are right where you belong."

I then close my eyes, and he sings his lullaby to me, causing me to drift away, into a dreamy sleep, something I haven't been able to do in months.

CHAPTER 25

BRADLEY

The sun is shining bright, and the leaves are turning colors. Reds, oranges, and yellows throughout the parks and squares. I finally have most of my strength back, so I decide to take a run while the girls are asleep.

Things have improved with Amelia and me. I think I finally gained her trust in me and our relationship. It was a task, but I convinced her that I was never leaving her.

Annabelle is growing so fast, and Amelia is great with her. She's a natural-born mother and giver to my baby girl. She treats her like her own, and I couldn't be happier.

Lately, my father has been drifting into my mind. For years I never gave two shits about him leaving us, but now that my mother is gone, I need to know what the fascination of beating women gave him. I want to know why taking someone's pride and joy is a drug to him. I want him to know that I turned out better than him. That I could never put a finger on my daughter or on Amelia for my pleasure to watch them cry. I don't get why men think it's okay to destroy the very thing that brings us into this world because, without them, we're nothing.

I wonder where he is. I wonder where he's been all this time and what he's been doing. I continue to run through the squares of Savannah when a police officer pulls up next to me, rolls his windows down and glances over his shades.

Sometimes I forget I'm in the South, and they don't expect Black men to be running in the downtown area unless they stole something. Which is the most ridiculous shit I've ever heard.

I'm pretty sure someone called on me, probably because I look '*suspicious*' in their eyes.

I pull out my air pods and stop on the sidewalk. I pull my grey hoodie off my head so he can clearly see who I am.

"Hello, Officer."

"Good morning. It's a beautiful day for a run in Savannah."

"Yes, it is," trying to reframe from catching an attitude.

"I've never seen you in this area before. Are you new to town?"

"Yes, my fiancé and I live on Broughton Street."

"Really?"

"Yes." Yes, really, asshole. I hate racist fuckers like this. I guess a Black man can't afford to live in the downtown area either. What a fucking joke.

Calm down, Brad. Fucking calm down, he may not be a racist at all. I might just be overreacting with all the shit I've been dealing with.

Putting his vehicle in park and getting out, "Well, the reason I stopped you is because someone called us. Do you have ID?" I guess I'm not overreacting.

Good thing I carry my ID at all times. Don't want to give him any reason to fuck with me.

"Yes, it's in my back pocket." I reach in my back pocket, watching him put his hand on his gun. I move as slowly as possible, so I don't give him any reason to feel threatened by me. "Here you go, officer."

He takes my ID and examines it like it's fake or something. "It says that you live near Forsyth Park."

"I have a house there too." I look at his nameplate to make sure I remember who he is. L. Wilson.

"I see. Stay put. If everything checks out, you are free to go."

I'm pretty sure I was free to go the moment he stopped me, but I don't want to give him the satisfaction of chasing me and gunning me down in these streets for no reason. After a while, he comes back with my ID. On-lookers watching our exchange. I wave politely. Glancing the other way, they continue running.

"Here, Mr. Philips. Everything checks out. You have a nice day."

"Thank you, Officer Wilson. You have a nice day as well," I say with obvious disdain and sarcasm in my tone. I can't stand this type of double standard. How people use the system to hurt others. The cop in me wants so badly to continue to strive for change, but my heart and mind can't take the audacity of people anymore.

I turn and continue to jog back home, no longer interested in running.

Welcome to the South, boy. You reckon you ain't from around here? That is all I heard when that son of a bitch started talking to me. I can't believe that we are still subjected to discrimination and racism in this day and age. But, Officer Wilson, you will find out who I am.

I make it back to the loft when greeted by my lovely fiancé. Flushing all those thoughts from my mind and easing my anger.

It's about time she becomes my wife.

"Good Morning, babe. How was your run?"

"It was enlightening and refreshing." I dare not tell her I was stopped by the police because I was running while being Black.

"Wow, nice choice of words," she deadpans.

"I should think so. I have a question for you," changing the subject.

"Shoot."

"How do you feel about having a small wedding in your sister's backyard with our family and closest friends?"

"That's a great idea!" She exclaims. "I've always wanted to get married in the backyard of my childhood home. When should we do this?"

"As soon as possible. I'm ready for you to be Mrs. Philips and start our family now," wrapping my arms around her tiny waist. I love this woman so much.

"Okay, but it may take a little time to get everyone to come, and I have to get a dress. I will need help setting up the backyard..." she rambles on, panic in her voice.

"Baby, I'm here to help with anything that needs to be done. I'm sure I can get Ryan and Jason to help as well."

She looks into my eyes with dread in her gaze. "Are you talking this weekend or like six months from now?"

"If I can marry you today, I would. But I also know that you have an opinion in the matter."

"Okay, let me talk with my sister, and I can give you a day that we can do this. I want to be your wife more than anything, and I want to be a mother to Annabelle."

"But, I also don't want to rush things, if I don't have to."

"I understand. Let's do this, if we can pull it off, let's go for it. If not, we can shoot for a later date. How does that sound?"

"Sounds good to me, but—."

"No buts, please no more issues," she pleads.

"Nothing like that. I just want you to be happy. That's all."

"I am. I do have a question though."

"Shoot."

"Is it okay with you if I adopt her?"

"Yes, of course. I want that more than anything too. I want us to be a family, and I want to add to our family. I'm not practicing for the hell of it," smacking her thick ass.

I pick her up and twirl her around. Finally, she starts laughing, and the pure happiness on her face is what I strive for every day.

"Okay, okay. Put me down. I have to make some phone calls if this is going to happen. Shoot, I need to get you a ring as well. I have so much to do. I will take Annabelle with me, and you can have some free time."

"Okay, babe." I kiss her on the forehead and set her down.

"There's breakfast in the microwave and fresh coffee in the pot," she says as she runs into the bedroom.

I turn on the microwave and grab a coffee mug out of the cabinet. I pour a little creamer and some hot coffee into the tumbler. I then take a sip leaning against the counter, absorbing everything around me.

My life has really changed for the good. I've been through some rough shit, but it has really shaped me into the person I am today. Which brings me back to this morning.

When will this type of discrimination end? Yes, the cop can say he was just doing his job, but when does it become a crime for a Black man to jog in his own neighborhood? I see White people do it every day, hell, at least ten passed by us during the subject stop and not once does it matter if they run, walk, or even crawl. This shit has to end.

And to think of it, I need to make a phone call to Ryan. It's time to get rid of Claire if it hasn't been done already.

I grab my phone and get my food out of the microwave. Amelia made grits, eggs, and bacon for breakfast. I can really get used to this.

I dial Ryan's number.

"Hey Brad, how's it going?"

"As well as can be. I can actually jog now without losing my breath."

"That's progress."

"Yeah, which leads me to my next question."

"Shoot."

"I'll be ready to come back to work in another couple of weeks. Has Claire left the office yet?"

"Hell yeah! We got rid of her the second we found out she was responsible for what happened. Megan took care of everything. You will have a new assistant by the time you come back. We got you, man. You and Amelia are family."

"Thanks, Ryan. That means a lot to me. I have another request."

"What's up?"

"Will you be my best man?"

"Shit yeah. I thought you'd never ask. I got you, bro. When we doing this?"

"As soon as Amelia gets confirmation on having it at her sister's home."

"Oh, man. When Jason and Lily got married there, it was like a fucking fairytale or some shit like that. I give it to them; they know how to throw a wedding."

"Good, that's what I'm hoping for. I don't know how to explain it. It's like I can't live or breathe without Amelia being a part of my life. And she's so good with Annabelle. I love her, man."

"Oh, we know. We all know. Amelia is a special person, and you two will be great together. Congratulation, man."

"Thanks."

"Hey, don't worry about the office. We got you. I've closed all of your open accounts and checked on your new accounts. They are doing well. Take care of yourself and Amelia and that sweet girl of yours. If you need anything else, just let me know."

"There is something else."

"What's up?"

"I would like to take Amelia somewhere nice for our honeymoon. Do you have any suggestions?"

"Absolutely. I own property in several countries, but my favorite is in the Philippines. Do you have a passport?"

"Sure do!"

"I will make the arrangements. That will be a gift to you from Kimberly and me. So don't worry about anything. I got this."

"Man, you don't have to do that."

"I know! That's why I'm doing it."

"Thanks, man. That means a lot."

"Family, bro. Family."

We then hang up, and I finish eating my breakfast. Amelia comes out of the room with curly hair, just like I like it, a yellow sundress, and sexy strappy sandals. Annabelle has a yellow dress on as well, with her hair done in pigtails with yellow bows.

"My god, y'all are a breath of fresh air. My girls look exceptional."

"Thanks, babe. We're headed to my sisters and then a couple of boutiques. If there's anything you need, just let me know."

"Okay, baby. Thanks." She wraps her free hand around my neck and kisses me softly. When we touch, that spark I always feel runs through me like a current of electricity running through a house. She sets me on fire, making me want to bend her over and fuck the shit out of her every moment of the day. But then, she pulls away, and I feel lost without her touch.

Pure torture every time we're apart. "Love you."

"Love you too."

CHAPTER 26

AMELIA

*A*fter helping with two weddings and now planning my own, you would think I would be a pro by now. Nope, I'm a blubbering mess. Everything has to be perfect. This is our day, and we have been through so much; we need this. Lily, Jess, Kim, and I are sitting in the kitchen of my childhood home. But it's not the same. Lily and Jason made some changes, and it looks incredible. The whole house has a modern feel to it. We are sitting around the island that can fit at least twenty people. It has a beautiful grey granite top with unique rustic bar height stools. My sister outdid herself with the renovations. She can do this as a career. She has always been so artistic.

"Amelia. Calm the hell down. We got this. Hell, you can get married this weekend at the rate we're going," Kim blurts out.

"I just want everything to be perfect. You know what I'm saying."

"Yes, we know. But, trust me, not everything is perfect, but your perfection will be different from everyone else's," says Lily.

"Look, we ordered the flowers to go along with that massive garden outback. We have a hundred chairs that we really don't need. You got this amazing ring for Brad and your dress, well, that dress will bring him to his knees," says Dianella while sipping on her wine.

"Okay, okay. Y'all are all ganging up on me. You know I'm a perfectionist. I need everything to go as planned," I confess.

"Yes, we know." They all singsong in unison. Then, we all burst out laughing.

Kim pulls something out of her purse and hands it over to me. "I got you a little something to use with Brad."

"Oh, okay. What is it?" I reach for it apprehensively. Kim always has something up her sleeve.

"Just open the damn thing."

"Okay, okay." I open the package and find a vibrator sitting in my hands. I drop it on the floor, almost afraid to touch it again. "What the hell, Kim?" I shout.

Kim laughs at me and gets down to pick the dick-shaped vibrator up. "Trust me, when you use this thing with Brad, he will be calling your name out from the tops of all the damn mountains."

"Seriously, Kim?" Lily chastise. "She was a virgin just a week ago. You can't throw her into the deep end and expect her to swim."

"Yes, I can, and she will lap that sexy god up in seconds with this toy right here." She swings it over her head like a propeller on a helicopter.

I grab the dick toy out of her hand and shove it in my purse. I roll my eyes at her and turn to Lily and Dianella. "Thank you for your help. I really do appreciate it," I emphasize, rolling my eyes at Kim.

"Of course, honey. We will always be here for you. You know that, right" Lily says. Her motherly instinct kicking in.

I hear the kids playing in the living room, the triplets, Annabelle, and Kim's son, RJ. Wow, I'm about to be a mother and a wife. I'm not scared, but I feel a little overwhelmed. I did not see my life turning out like this six months ago, but I wouldn't have it any other way.

Lily grabs my hand and squeezes it gently, probably noticing my mood change. "You will be a wonderful mother to Annabelle and an amazing wife to Bradley. I know this is a lot, but I've watched you over the years, and you're ready. I've never seen you look at anyone the way you look at Bradley. You two are meant for each other," simplifying the very thoughts I was having.

"You really think so?"

"Absolutely. That man loves you and will put you before anyone else, well, except Annabelle. But that is to be expected from a father, a single father at that. You are a strong, loving person and Bradley is lucky to have you in his life. I just wish mom and dad could be here to see you now."

"I wish they were too," squeezing her hand right back, tears whelming up behind my eyelids.

"Okay, okay. Enough of the sad shit. This is supposed to be a happy moment. Reverend Carter said he would officiate the wedding. I think we got this shit. Next weekend you will be Mrs. Bradley Philips," Dianella announces.

Changing the subject, "Hey, how are you and Lenny doing?" I ask. Dianella's face turns dark and worrisome at the mention of his name. "Sweetie, is everything okay? He's not hurting you, is he?" concern etched in my features.

"Oh, no. Nothing like that. I just found out he has this whole other life that I knew nothing about, and I'm concerned. That's all."

"What life is that? He's not doing illegal shit, is he?" Kim asks.

"Define illegal."

"Are you fucking kidding me, Dianella?" Kim scowls.

"Hold on. Just give her a second to explain. Maybe it's not as bad as we think," Lily suggests.

"I think he used to sell drugs or something because some scary guys have been around lately. At first, Lenny told me not to worry about it. Probably because he knows my brother is a cop. But then I started getting a bad feeling. I think he used to do it and tried to get out, but these people won't let him out."

"Dianella Hall. Listen to me and listen to me good. Lily and I both dealt with that type of world working the streets. It's nothing to mess around with. If Lenny is fucked up in some shit, you need to let him go. He will bring you down with him, and that is not a place you want to be. You have a business, for god's sake. You're going to school, and you're trying to get your license for culinary school. Do you want to lose all of that for some thug?" Kim asks.

"Wait a minute; he is not a thug," Dianella defends. "Let me get you straight on that first. And he's trying to get out. I just don't know how he can. I really like this guy, and I think he really likes me."

"Dianella, listen to yourself. This guy used to be the very thing that we all fought against while working in the department. Hell, your brother still is, and you just, what? Just want to say fuck it all, I'm going to join the underworld. Seriously," Kim snaps, throwing her hands up with disdain in every word.

"Kim, leave her alone. She came to us because she wants our support, not belittle her or berate her." I get up, and I wrap my arms around Dianella's shoulders. "Dianella, you know I love you and will do anything for you. You are my sister, and you would do the very same thing to one of us if we came to you with this information. We are just concerned like you are. We don't want to see anything happen to you or your business. We are here for you and will do anything to protect you. I will not tell you who to love, but I will tell you to be careful. The same words you told me when I found Bradley."

"Thank you, Amelia. That means a lot to me," Dianella admits with tears streaming down her face. "And Kim, I know you mean well, and I hear everything you're saying. I just want to make sure I'm doing the right thing."

"That's all I ask," Kim confesses, defeating from the obvious elephant in the room.

"Okay, everyone. Group hug," Lily announces.

"How convenient. You sit there watching this unfold and come and save the day at the bitter end," I say, shaking my head.

We all burst out laughing. "Mama bear at her best," Lily snickers.

We then all stand and hug each other. "To Family."

"To Family," we all toast together.

～

My life is evolving before my eyes, and I sometimes wonder how I even got here? I was a nice quiet girl who just wanted to remain under the radar, and then I met Bradley, and that sweet innocent, quiet girl no longer exits. I'm stronger than I ever thought I would ever be. Hell, I was strong as a young child, but I never really voiced my opinion on something or put myself in harm's way to help another. And now look at me.

I'm about to be a wife to a man who adores me and a mother to a beautiful baby girl who looks up to me. Me. She chose me to look up to, and I have to be there for her no matter if she's my blood or not. She will be my daughter, and I will treat her as such.

Annabelle and I pull up in the garage after a long day. I got a lot accomplished, but I'm dead tired. I park the SUV and get Annabelle out of her car seat. She's already fast asleep and hasn't budged a muscle when picking her up. She must have had a wonderful time with her cousins.

I smile to myself because it's such a wonderful feeling to be starting a family now. I walk inside the mudroom, and I'm automatically hit with a fantastic smell from the kitchen.

"Oh my gosh, that smells delectable. What are you cooking?" I walk into the kitchen, and I am greeted by Bradley with a soft kiss and a glass of wine. He grabs Annabelle out of my arms and turns to head to her playpen. Shortly later, he returns with the most gorgeous smile, showing off his perfectly white teeth. God, I love this man. He's absolutely the most alluring man I've ever encountered. When I see his eyes, I know without a doubt I'm making the right decision to have this strong Black man in my life and in my future.

"We're having shrimp and grits for dinner. It's a beautiful fall evening, and I was hoping we would share dinner together on the balcony?"

"Of course. It's nice to come home to a sexy man and a home-cooked meal after a long day."

"I know you were pretty busy getting ready for the wedding, and I wanted to do something to let you know that I appreciate you and everything you have done and will do for our family."

"Seriously, after the day I had, I need a home-cooked meal, a glass of wine, and a foot massage... I'm just saying," I shrug my shoulders, both of us laughing.

"Good, now go outside, sit and relax. I will bring your dinner to you. Be sure to take your wine as well. And I'll prepare to love on those feet of mine," he winks at me.

"Now you're talking!"

I place my purse on the counter, head to the balcony, and sit in one of the lounge chairs with my wine in hand. The sun is setting; the sky is filled with red, purple, and orange rays drifting around the downtown area. People are still out and about shopping and having dinner in the many local shops on Broughton Street. Again, I see why Jason fell in love with this loft. You get a feel of the nightlife and privacy at your fingertips.

Bradley comes towards me with a serving tray of two bowls of shrimp and grits. He sets it on the coffee table and sits next to me.

"This lighting is stunning tonight."

"Yes, it is." He hands me a bowl, and I put my wine glass down after taking another sip. Even though I was headed straight for the shower and then bed, I really needed this. This is a nice change of pace. I can really get used to this.

Bradley says the blessings, and then we take a bite of his masterpiece.

Oh. My. Gosh.

"This is effing amazing," I say with a mouth full of food, trying not to curse anymore. "Where in the world did you learn how to make shrimp and grits like this?"

"My mom taught me everything she knew. She always said a man should know his way around a kitchen. A sorry man sits and waits for someone else to serve him."

"Well, thank God for Mrs. Philips. She taught you well." I take several more bites when Bradley speaks again.

"Babe, I've been thinking." Uh, oh. It must be severe. His tone has slightly shifted to serious. Is this why he's trying to butter me up? The other shoe about to come crashing down.

"What is it? Is everything okay?' I ask with concern in my tone, setting my fork down.

"Yes, everything's okay. Nothing like that. I just been thinking about looking for my biological father. I have so many questions that I would like to have answers for."

"Wow, are you sure about that? I mean, where will you start?" A little surprised. This came out of left field, catching me completely off guard.

"Not sure, but I was thinking about hiring someone to track him down."

"Well, yeah, that makes sense. If you do find him, what do you want to know?" I ask, genuinely curious.

"I want to know why more than anything. I don't want or need anything from him. I just want to know what the fascination was with beating my mother. He not only forced me to grow up without a father figure in my life, but he also left my mother alone to fend for herself and an impressionable young boy to raise."

"I get it, but do you think this will add more problems to what we already have."

"What do you mean?"

"Well, most men who abandon their family or force their family to leave them because of fear are cowards. They want you to suffer because they are suffering. And what if he's still that same hateful person? Do you want that type of person around Annabelle?"

"Of course not; I will never bring him around you or Annabelle unless I know it's safe. So I get what you're saying, but I still have so much of my life missing, and I just want answers."

"I get it. Trust me, I know more than anyone wanting to get guidance from your parents or ask them as much as possible if you had the opportunity. I want that every day of my life, but I also understand now, more than ever, there are some really fucked up people out there who call themselves parents, and it's best to leave those types of evils right where they are. You, sir, have turned into an exceptional and remarkable young man and father. You are the very thing people wish for and hope for. Don't get me wrong, I will support you in any decision you make, but I also have to speak my opinion on the matter, and I think it's a bad idea."

"Okay, babe. I respect your opinion and will consider your opinion and the safety of you and Annabelle. If I find him and meet with him, I will do it alone, so I don't subject you or Annabelle to disrespect or harm."

"No, I want to be there with you if you decide; I just don't think it's a good idea. That's all."

"Fair enough."

CHAPTER 27

BRADLEY

*A*melia may be right about this being a bad idea, but I still need to find out where my father is and why he did what he did. This is something I have to do, and I will do.

I'm sitting in my office at work, really not doing anything. Ryan took care of most of my accounts while I was out, so there really isn't any reason for me to be here, but I just want my life back. I want to be back on my feet, doing what I love and desire.

The other day drifts back into my mind. Officer Wilson. I pick up the phone and call the person I think can help.

"Hey Jason, you got a minute to discuss something?"

"Sure. Go ahead."

"The other day, I was jogging in the downtown area, and I was stopped by an Officer Wilson. He said he stopped me because someone called and said I didn't belong in the area, and I looked suspicious. Now, granted, I ran with a hoodie over my head and air pods in my ears, but I was on the sidewalk, obeying all pedestrian laws and crossing intersections. It wasn't so much of him stopping me; it was the way he made me feel when he stopped me. He questioned me even being able to afford to live on Broughton Street or even the downtown area."

"I see. You're not the only person who has tried to make a complaint against this officer."

"Really. So, you're saying that others have complained about the same thing, and nothing has been done?"

"Yeah, that's what I'm saying. But, with this new information, I will take care of it. Are you willing to make a formal complaint in reference to the officer?"

"Absolutely! That type of behavior doesn't ever need to happen to anyone. No one should feel like they are treated differently or beneath them in any way."

"Did you tell him you were a cop for ten years?"

"Should I have to?" I spit out with obvious cattiness in my tone.

"Sorry, man, I didn't mean any offense. I just know when you're a cop or an ex-cop, officers will treat you differently.'

"That shouldn't be the case. Whether I'm a cop or not, I should not be treated any differently than the white men and women who run, jog, or walk down the same streets as I do. It's wrong, and I won't stand for that type of behavior from anyone, Black, White, Hispanic, or Asian."

"Received wholeheartedly. I will start the complaint process. And I'm sorry you were treated that way. I don't always understand the mistreatment because I never treated people any differently, but I have witnessed it with my wife, and it pisses me off how someone can treat another person differently because of the color of their skin. My wife is the sweetest person I know, and she would never hurt anyone on purpose. Now, don't get me wrong, she will slaughter you from neck to navel if she has to, but she will never deliberately hurt someone because of how they look, and I wouldn't do it either."

"I know, bro. But not everyone thinks or acts like you. So it's up to you and me to check that type of behavior."

"Absolutely. I got your back, and something will be done about it."

"Thanks. I appreciate your help. Oh, wait. I have another question."

"What's up?"

"I want to find out where my father is? Do you know any good PIs that could help with that?"

"Yes, well, she used to be a PI before she became the police and then quit the force, but she still does work for the police department on the side."

"Who?"

"Kim Taylor, Ryan's wife."

"Oh, I didn't know that."

"Yeah. She's really good at finding people and doing a complete background history on them. So I'm sure she will help with whatever you need."

"Thanks, man. I will reach out to Ryan."

"Any time. How is the planning for the wedding going? Lily told me that y'all want to have it in the backyard of our home."

"Yeah. Amelia really wants to feel connected to her parents, and that would be a way to honor them, to be closer to them."

"Our home is your home. Whatever you need, just let us know."

"Thanks, man. Everyone has been very supportive in everything."

"That's what family does."

We then hang up, and I call Ryan into my office.

"Hey Ryan, can I speak to you about something really quick?"

"Sure. I will be right in. Just give me a sec. I have to close this account."

"Sure."

A moment later, Ryan strolls into my office with a tailored navy-blue suit, light blue shirt, and some peanut butter Cole Haans. Now that I think about it, I need to get myself a new wardrobe.

"Hey, what's up?" He asks.

"I want to find out where my father is, and I was told that your wife, Kim, can help me out."

"Yeah, she's really good at finding people. She's the one that found Lily when she was kidnapped and was able to assist with bringing down an entire sex trafficking operation."

"Holy shit, I had no idea."

"Yeah. She's pretty awesome. And I'm sure she'll assist you with whatever you need."

"Thanks, man. I wanted to get your permission first before I reach out to her. Gotta give that respect."

"Thanks. I appreciate it. What are you doing for lunch today?"

"I hadn't really thought about it. Amelia is heading to Lily's to prepare for the wedding, so I'm free. What did you have in mind?"

"Some of the guys and I would like to take you to lunch and help with the tux."

I was not expecting that at all. Well, I guess I really hadn't thought about it either. "Sure. That would be great. I was just going to wear one of my suits in the closet."

"You are a millionaire now. It's time to dress and act like it. Besides, you're making plenty of money with these accounts."

"Yeah, I guess you're right. I was just thinking about redoing my wardrobe. I guess now is as good as any."

"Let's go. We will have lunch at the Marshall's House and then head to my tailor to get you fitted for a whole new wardrobe. The girls already did this for Amelia. I will be damned if they had one up on us," we chuckle and head out. "Megan, can you hold all of our calls? We're headed out for an extended lunch," Ryan explains, turning around.

"Yes, sir. Enjoy."

"Also, you're invited to our wedding, Mrs. Megan. We would love to have you there," I announced as we walked out.

"Thank you, Mr. Bradley. I will be there." I smile at her and then follow Ryan out to the car. He's driving a Rolls-Royce Culling, white in color with peanut butter leather interior. The car is fly as hell and it's about time I get my dream car.

"We're meeting Jason and a couple of guys from the police department."

"Cool." We both get into the car and head to Broughton Street. We pull up to the front entrance, and Ryan hands over his keys to the valet. I see him slip a hundred-dollar bill to the gentleman. He always gives and does for others. That is the person I want to be. I want to bring someone under my wing, just like Ryan did for me. He's not that much older than me, but I still respect him as a mentor and brother.

We walk in and we're immediately welcomed by the hostess. "Good Afternoon Mr. Ryan. We have your table ready. Please follow me. Some of your party has already arrived."

"Thank you, Jackie. I appreciate it," Ryan says.

We arrive at our seats, and I see Jason, some of the detectives that work with him, and showed up at the house, and I see the officer who stopped me the other day.

What the fuck is he doing here?

He stands up to greet me. "Before you say anything, I want to say sorry, man. I had no idea that I was behaving in such a way, and it was finally brought to my attention."

"You mean to tell me no one has ever told you that you were racially profiling against Black men?"

"No. It was never brought to my attention, and I didn't realize that's what I was doing. I would have done something about it if I'd known, and I'm doing it now. I work with a great group of guys, and I never want them to feel that I don't respect them or judge them based on the color of their skin."

"I understand, but something still needs to be done about this. First, we need to find out who's sweeping this type of behavior under the rug, and we need to address that person. You also need to under-stand that you need to reevaluate your morals and ethics if you thought it was okay to stop me and question me because I scared a person just by jogging in my neighborhood. Someone shouldn't have to come to you and tell you it's wrong. You should already know it's wrong."

"You're right. I should have known," not blinking an eye, "which is wrong on so many levels. What I was taught should never be different than what I present. Thankfully, we no longer live in that environment, and I take responsibility for my actions."

"That's certainly a start."

"Did I just walk into something?" Ryan quips cautiously.

"We had a misunderstanding earlier, and hopefully, it's taken care of now," I glance towards Officer Wilson.

"Yes, of course. I'm taking care of it now," he agrees with a slightly harsher tone.

Hell, I didn't mean to offend the dude, but he needs to turn in that badge if he's easily offended.

We all sit down at the round table near the window. The Marshall's House is a historical building accented with red Savannah brick and green shutters. It may be an old building, but they sure did renovate the inside to look like a high-end sophisticated modern style. Amelia would love this type of culture and design.

"So, how does it feel?" Jason asks.

"How does what feel?" I question back, taking a sip of my water.

"Married life, of course."

"Well, I'm not married yet, but I can say that it's the second-best decision I ever made."

"And the first?"

"Having my daughter. These two women have shaped my life to be a better man. Hell, my mother had a hand in that, and without the three of them, I would probably be running the streets doing nothing with my life. I knew I wanted to marry Amelia the second I saw her with my daughter. The way they clicked immediately; it was something to see and witness."

"How about you?" I asked Jason.

"Marrying Lily was the best decision I've made as well. She made me stronger, opened my whole heart, and gave birth to the three most precious things God could have blessed us with, our two boys and daddy's baby girl," Jason says with a smile on his face.

"And you, Ryan?" I ask.

"Do you even have to ask that question? My wife and our son are the light of my life. Without them, I'm nothing. My life has always been about making my parents proud and using my privilege to do better with society. Now, I have something to work even harder for and leave a legacy that will follow for many years."

"Damn, I had no idea marrying someone could change your life completely like that," Officer Wilson mentions.

"Marrying the right person will change you," Jason corrects. "You can't just marry just anyone in hopes that it will make a difference. Getting to know a person down to their very soul and knowing without a doubt that you would do anything in your power to protect that person and vice-versa will change you completely."

"I haven't found that at all," Officer Wilson admits.

"You will, Lamonte. You will," Jason says.

"Wait, your name is Lamonte?" I probe.

"Yeah, believe it or not, my mother is Black, and my father is White. I know I look White, but I'm actually mixed."

"Wow, I would have never guessed. I learn something new every day."

"And so, do I," Lamonte agrees. "So do I."

"Can I get y'all something to drink?" the waitress asks us.

"Yes, bring us a round of Tennessee Mule and some appetizers for the table," Ryan announces.

"Is that it?" the waitress asks.

"For now. Thank you," Ryan answers.

"Okay, I'll be back with your drinks."

"Thank you," Ryan complements.

"So, Brad, how are you holding up with everything else? It hasn't been easy these past couple of months," Jason changes the subject.

"You're right; it hasn't been easy, but Amelia and all of you have been great, and I couldn't have asked for a better family to be a part of. I think I was more worried about Amelia than myself."

"Why do you say that?" Jason asks with concern in his tone.

"Well, she lost both of her parents, almost lost her sister and best friend, and almost lost me. And yet, she was by my side every day and night, praying over me. She endured a lot, and I just want to make sure she's okay, more so than me."

"She's a strong girl. Hell, all of our women are. You will soon discover that these women are not like most. It's best to let them thrive in their strength and be there when they need you," Ryan counters. "It's a lot to deal with, but you both will find peace with time."

"Yes, I know." Finally, the waitress comes back with our drinks.

"Drinks are served. Your appetizers will be ready in just a moment."

"Thank you. Uh, miss, what is your name?" I ask.

"Ah, yes. My name is Stephanie."

"Thank you, Stephanie."

"You're welcome. Can I get you anything else?"

"No, ma'am. I think that will be it for now." She then walks away.

"Hey, Nate. You're not getting off that easy. How are you and Renee doing?" Jason asks.

"We're doing good. She wants to buy a new house," Nate announces. Nathaniel Johnson has been a client of Ryan's for years. He works at the police department as well. I believe a captain for their training unit.

"What's wrong with the house y'all are in now?"

"Well, it was the house of mine and my ex-wife. She wants to be in her own house and put a piece of her in it."

"Ah, I see. She's right, you know," Ryan points out.

"Yeah, I know. I've just been pushing back a little."

"Keep pushing, and you'll push her right out the damn house and marriage. So keep fucking up," Jason spits out, chuckling between sips of water.

"Okay, okay. I will make it right, okay."

"You don't have to convince us. You need to crawl back on your knees, apologize, and give that woman what she wants. Happy house makes a happy wife," Jason sings.

"You have a beautiful young Black woman. Keep pissing her off, and someone will take her off your hands. You didn't learn from the first marriage? Damn man," Ryan says, shaking his head.

"Fuck, I said I would take care of it. Get off my back."

"We just making sure you understand. Some other dick will be in that tight pussy, and you will be drowning in sorrow when you finally realize you fucked up. Hell, you got the money. So stop being a pussy," Jason snaps.

"Fuck you, Hall. Ain't no motherfucker will be fucking my wife," Nate spits out.

"You keep fucking up, and Lamonte here will have a field day with her," Jason says, patting Lamonte on the back, clearly taunting Nate.

"Hey, don't bring me in the middle of this shit. I'm not ready for a relationship anyway," Lamonte says, throwing his hands up.

"You will when you find the right one. Look at all of us. We said the same thing and now look at us. Married with kids," Ryan says with a chuckle.

We all burst out laughing. I'm enjoying this. I really haven't had men to look up to. This is great. Our appetizers finally come, and we become silent, too busy eating than talking, which is fine with me. I was starving for some reason.

Ryan pulls the tab and pays for our lunch. He's a pretty decent guy. I'm actually stoked I came. These guys are cool as shit. Next, we head to Ryan's tailor shop. Who would have known he was the face of the south.

We stand in front of Joseph's Clothier on Broughton Street, wondering if this is a good idea. I need to talk to Amelia first. She has no idea I'm about to spend a shit load of money on clothes and shoes. I pull out my phone and dial her number.

"I see you're pussy-whipped already," Jason mocks.

"Not pussy-whipped, respectable to my fiancé. She needs to know that I'm about to spend a ton of money."

"Don't listen to that asshole. He does the same thing. Talk with your wife. Communication is key in every relationship," Ryan says.

She answers after a couple of rings. "Hey babe, what's up?"

"Nothing much. The guys and I are about to go shopping for a tux for the wedding and pick up a few more things."

"Okay, babe. Thanks for telling me, but it's your money. You can spend it however you like."

"No, I can't. It's our money, and I want to let you know everything that I'm doing so we can budget accordingly."

"Yeah, you're right. I probably should tell you I spent a little over fifty thousand on the wedding already," flabbergasted, she spent way too much money. "Sorry I didn't tell you. I'm just not used to answering to someone about finances other than my financial advisor. To think of it, it should be you and not Ryan." Dead silence over the phone. I'm fucking speechless.

"Bradley, are you still there?"

"Um, yeah, no, Ryan is great. We can sit down together with him and let him manage our accounts. That way, we can have an outside opinion on our expenditures."

"I guess you're right. We can talk about it later. I'm out with the girls and have the kids with us. Enjoy your shopping. You deserve it."

"Thanks, baby. Love you," still a little shocked. How can she spend that kind of money so easily, without a second thought?

"Love you too." She then hangs up. We have a lot to talk about now that I think about it.

"Hey, man. Are you ready?" Nate asks.

"Yeah. Ready."

"Hi Kim, how are you?" I decided to call Kim to assist me with finding my father. Everyone says she's the best at what she does.

"I'm good. Just been pretty busy with the new Safe Haven for battered women. What can I do for you?"

"Well, if you aren't extremely busy, I was hoping you could help me with something?"

"What's that?"

"I want to find my father, and Ryan said you're the best at finding people who don't want to be found."

"Sure, I can help with that. Do you have his name and date of birth?"

"Well…Uh…wait. Yes, I do. It should be on my birth certificate. I will have to look through my files at home."

"If you can get me that, it would go a lot faster with finding him."

"Okay. Thanks, Kim."

"Anytime. Besides, Amelia will kill me if I don't help," she snickers to herself over the phone.

"Yeah, my fiancé is not a big fan of me finding him, but she is supporting me."

"That's Amelia. Always supporting someone or something."

"Yeah, that's why I fell in love with her."

"Oh, so it wasn't the incredible sex," she quips.

We both burst out laughing. "What happens behind closed doors is our business."

"Yeah, whatever you say."

We then hang up; I leave the office and head home. It's been a long day, and I just want to play with my daughter and drink wine with my fiancé.

I pull up in the garage and head to the elevator. I get in and realize this elevator doesn't have music. Maybe we can implement that with the HOA. I walk inside the loft and hear music coming from Amelia's dance studio. I look around, and I see dinner has already been made and sitting on the stove. I walk through the kitchen and head towards the dance studio. I haven't actually seen her dance before because we had so much going on. I stop at the glass door and glance through.

My God, she's actually a full-on Black ballerina. She's gliding across the floor effortlessly, and her body shows emotion I've never witnessed before. She's like a swan floating in the pond, a bird drifting in the wind. She's absolutely mesmerizing. She stops abruptly and begins to spin on her tippy toes, and then she lifts one of her legs, and her sheer dress flows around her like a colorful flower roaming in the sky. I see her passion, obsession, and love for dance and movement in this very moment. She's telling a story, and we are all here to witness the tale. I see Annabelle in the corner, watching her with eyes so big. She's as fascinated with Amelia as I am. Then, she slows down with her spinning and graceful falls to the floor with a soothing purpose. I can watch her all day.

Her alarm goes off, and she goes to turn the music off. No, she can't stop. I want to see more. I open the door and enter the dance studio.

"Baby, why did you stop. That was amazing."

She looks up, startled. I thinks she's surprised that I saw her dancing. "Oh, I didn't know you were home. I wanted dinner to be done before you arrived."

"Forget dinner. I want to see more of that. I had no idea you could dance like that. I know you told me you love to dance, but damn.

That was breathtaking." She begins to blush as she picks up Annabelle from her play area.

"Thank you, babe; I will dance more often, I have a recital coming up soon, I've just been preoccupied with everything going on, and besides, Annabelle has to eat. I promise to dance for you later. Okay?" staring with pleading eyes.

"I will hold you to that promise. Here I'll take care of Annabelle while you clean up. Is there anything you need me to do with dinner?" I grab Annabelle from her arms, and Annabelle wraps her tiny arms around my neck.

"Hey, baby girl. Daddy, miss you."

"Da, da."

"No, everything is done. I just need to serve it. Go have a cold beer and sit on the balcony. I will bring the dinner out to you. Annabelle's dinner is in the microwave cooling off."

There's something going on there, but I don't push her. Amelia will be open with me in due time. But, there is something definitely on her mind and I will figure it out.

"Okay, baby. I will see you in a few." Annabelle and I walk out of the studio and head for the kitchen. I retrieve her dinner from the microwave, and I grab a beer out of the fridge. I definitely need one of these right about now. I head to the balcony and sit with Annabelle in my lap.

"Hey, baby girl. You've been holding out on me. Why didn't you tell me mommy could dance like that? She was amazing, wasn't she?" I question Annabelle, knowing she can't manage to respond with complete sentences.

"Ma, ma."

"Ah, yes, baby girl. Mommy is amazing."

"Thank you, babe. I appreciate that." Amelia walks out on the balcony with two plates in her hand. She's wearing a pair of black tights and a long off the shoulder shirt, with her hair in a messy bun. "I had no idea you never really saw me dance before. I will make sure that changes sooner than later."

"That's all I ask for," I agree. "Wow, dinner looks good, baby. Steak and broccoli. My favorite."

We both laugh, "Yes, I know."

After we say our blessings, I bring up the finances.

"Love?"

"Yes," she answers after chewing her steak.

"I think we should discuss our financial abilities."

"Okay. What do you want to know?"

"Well, do you want joint accounts or separate accounts?"

"I think we should have separate accounts for different responsibilities. Like a billing account and/or play account. I think both our names should be on all of our accounts. We will be family, and what is mine is yours, and what is yours is mine."

That was easy. "I agree. My mother left me over two hundred and fifty million, and she started a trust fund for Annabelle and any future children we will have."

"Yes, I remember," she quips. Something definitely bothering her. "I'm worth at least eighty-five million. This house is paid for already, and my car is paid for. Are there any bills outstanding on your end?"

"Actually, no. I rented the house on Drayton Street, and Ryan paid for my education. I own my car as well. It's a little outdated, but it serves the purpose I need. I'm thinking of getting another vehicle. You know my favorite is the S500."

"You should definitely get your dream car. You deserve it. So, we are worth over three hundred thirty-five million between the two of us. I think we should sit down with Ryan to see what we can invest in, what we should put in savings, and how much we should set aside for anything we want to get involved in."

"Sounds good to me. Do you want to continue living in this home, or do you want to purchase a home together?"

"I never really thought about it. I moved out of my childhood home to give Lily and Jason privacy, and it was time for me to be on my own. I never thought I would be getting married anytime soon or deciding to purchase a home. I'm okay with whatever decision we make together."

"I think we're fine here for now, but we may need more space if we're working to grow our family. I want you to be able to have your studio, and our kids have their own rooms."

"Yeah, okay. I agree," she shrugs her shoulders nonchalantly. There is seriously something going on. We finish our dinner and just sit watching Annabelle play with her toys on the balcony floor.

It's a gorgeous evening, and it's nowhere cold here like it is up north. I wish it could stay like this every night.

"Bradley, I have something to say." Here it goes. I knew something was on her mind.

"What's that, baby?" giving her the floor.

"I know I was a little harsh about you finding your father, and I want to apologize. Lately, I've been on edge, and I should not take it out on you."

"It's okay, Love. I get it. But, why are you on edge?" I question.

"I don't think I'm ready to talk about it yet."

"Know that I am here," not wanting to push her too much.

"I know."

By the way, I reached out to someone to help find my father," changing the subject. I know she's not ready for whatever it is, but she will be. "Now that I think about it, she asked me for his full name and date of birth. At the time, I didn't even realize I never knew what my father's name was. It should be on my birth certificate."

"Who did you reach out to?"

"Kim. Ryan said she's the best, and she's quick."

"Yeah, he's right. I forgot all about that. She did a wonderful job finding my sister when she went missing. I can't believe I didn't think of her when you asked," clearly beating herself up.

"We had a lot going on in the past couple of months. I'm just glad she's able to help. I don't know what we'll find out, but at least I can say I tried. Hell, he might tell me to fuck off. We don't really know. All I know is it will be a huge weight lifted off my shoulders."

"If I had the opportunity to say one thing to my parents and gave that opportunity up, I would be devastated. So, I'm actually proud of you for standing up, taking the lead of your life and your future. Most people would have shied away from the opportunity, especially if that parent was responsible for the abuse of another parent and you. But, you just watching or hearing is abuse on its own, and it's a miracle that you turned out totally different than your father."

"Yeah. I guess I really didn't think of it that way at all. I did turn out to be a good guy if I do say so myself."

We both laugh and finish drinking our wine.

"It sure is a beautiful night. I love this time of year."

"I do too."

My beautiful fiancé lay on our bed with her hair scattered across the pillow and her legs wide open for me to play with my toys. Yes, that pussy is one of my toys, and I will smell it, taste it, and play with it as much as I want to.

My dick throbbing harder just thinking about my mouth sucking that sweet pussy of mine.

"Amelia, you're so beautiful, so pure, and you're all mine. Baby, I want to see you touch yourself."

"Okay." She reaches down and opens her plump lips wide for me to see. She then glides her fingers over her clit, and I watch her pleasure herself, and it's a fucking turn on.

"Baby, fuck that pretty little pussy with your fingers. I want you to make yourself come." I grab my dick, and I stroke it with my hand.

"Like this baby?" she moans. I watch her insert two fingers in her pussy, just as I taught her. Her creamy essences soak around her fingers and slide down her ass. It's so fucking hot; it's making me harder and harder by the second.

"That's it, baby. Do it harder. I want you to come. I want to see you come all over those fingers of yours."

"Okay, babe." She then increases the speed, but then I see her reach for something behind her head. It's bright pink.

Holy fuck, she got a vibrator. She turns it on and places it on her clit. I see her clit perk up, and it's the most erotic thing I've ever witnessed from her. I've never used a vibrator before with someone. This is going to be interesting.

"Oh. My. Fucking. Gosh. This feels so good," she mummers softly.

"Baby, that's so hot. I didn't know you use a vibrator."

"Ah, shit. Bradley, I need you inside of me, please!" she begs.

Hell, I'm about to come my damn self just watching her with that vibrator. I climb on top of her and thrust my dick inside of her. Holy shit. I can feel the vibration as well. This is fucking interesting. More like fucking amazing.

"Holy shit, babe. That right there feels fucking awesome." I gather myself and try my damnedest to hold as long as possible. I thrust, and I thrust. Between this soaking wet pussy and that vibrating, this is the best experience I've ever had.

"Bradley, baby. I'm about to come. Please fuck me harder. Please."

I love it when she begs me to fuck her. I brace myself and pray I can hold on long enough to make her come, thrusting inside of her over and over, harder and harder. Our bodies smacking between thrusts.

"Oh my gosh. Yes, yes, yes. Right there, babe. Oh my god, I'm about to come."

"Fuck, I'm coming too, babe. Fuck, Amelia." I feel her grip my dick, and we both take a ride of a lifetime.

"SSShhhiiittt! Bradley. Fuck," she screams out between panting.

"Goddamnit! Amelia." She then turns off the vibrator, and I damn near collapse on top of her. I pull out once she releases my dick and rollover.

"Holy shit Amelia. That was fucking amazing. I've never done that before."

"Me neither. Kim is the one who told me I should use it with you. She bought it for me as a gift."

"Well, thank you, Kim. Fuck, we'll have to use that every time for now on."

We both laugh, and she cuddles up in my arms and rests her head on my chest. For a person who has been shot, I feel brand new.

"Bradley?"

"Yes, babe?"

"I'm glad I can experience new things with you."

"Hell, if it feels like that every time, I'll experience the world with you."

Laughing to ourselves, we drift to sleep.

CHAPTER 28

AMELIA

*I*t's been a week, and I already have butterflies fluttering in my stomach. My big day is approaching, and I'm so excited. I just wish my parents could be here to see me walk down that aisle with that beautiful dress. I wish my mother could give me encouraging advice for motherhood and being a wife. I know dad would approve of Bradley, but I just want to hear the words from his mouth. I might be overwhelmed with joy, but I'm also a little sad inside. I know Bradley has seen my mood change and I just hope he understands once I gather the strength to be open and honest with him.

I wonder what Lily felt when she was in this very moment. She's so much more robust and braver than I am. Lily has been my rock, and it's now time for me to be strong and courageous like her. She and my parents taught me everything I know.

I'm sitting on the balcony, the wind blowing, and birds are chirping. Annabelle is still sleeping, and so is Bradley. This moment in the morning, I have to myself to reflect on the past, the present, and the future. Drinking my coffee and absorbing what life has to offer, my phone rings. Wow, it's a little early, so I answer it. It might be important.

"Hello?"

"Hey, Amelia. Sorry to call so early, but I have some information Bradley might want to hear," Kim announces through the receiver.

"Oh, no. It's fine. Here, let me wake him up."

"Thanks, Amelia. I normally would not make you wake your husband-to-be, but you know how I am; when my mind is set on a mission, I follow it through until the very end."

"I know. Hold for just a minute. I'm walking into the house now." I walk towards the bedroom to wake Bradley up.

"Sitting on the balcony contemplating life again?" Kim asks.

"You know it." I enter the bedroom, and Bradley is still fast asleep. He must be exhausted. He never sleeps in like this.

"Babe?" I softly rub his shoulder, so I don't scare him. "Hey, babe?"

"Humph," he moans and yawns, rolling over. "Good morning, Sunshine," pulling me on top of him, kissing me on my neck.

"Good morning, babe; Kim is on the phone. She said she has some information for you." He sits up on the bed, releasing me, and I sit next to him. I put the phone on speaker.

"Kim, sweetie, I have you on speaker. So he can hear you."

"Thanks, babe. Okay, Bradley. I think I found your father," Bradley's eyes widen, and he sits with anticipation. "Please don't get too excited just yet; I have bad news for the first part. I found your father, but I think he passed away five years ago. He suffered from lung cancer; however, he had other children. You have two siblings, a sister and a brother. Your sister is one year younger than you. Her name is Charlotte. She lives in Jacksonville, Florida. She's a prosecutor for Duvall County Courthouse. Your brother's name is Wade. He lives in Atlanta, Georgia. He is three years younger than you. He is in his fourth year of college at Georgia University. He's studying Accounting. Go figure. I have their address and phone numbers if you want to make contact. It appears that their mother is still alive as well."

Bradley sits in the bed and doesn't make a sound. I think he's more stunned than anything by the information he just heard.

"Are you guys still there?" Kim asks, after a moment of silence.

"Uh, yeah. I think Bradley is stunned, speechless, absorbing the information you just gave him. We would love to have their numbers and address. Is there anything else?" I ask.

"Yes, I have their birth certificates, deeds for their home, college transcripts, and more."

"Good god, Kim. I had no idea you could get all that information that quick."

"Yep, I'm about that life, hacker life" she bursts out laughing.

"Thanks, Kim. I love you, and I will see you soon."

"Okay, babe. Love you too. Let me know if you need anything else."

"Sure thing." We then hung up.

I turn to face Bradley, who is still speechless, and I know he needs me more now than any time before. That was a lot of information to lay on him right now.

"Babe, are you okay?" he looks up at me and stares me into my eyes. Those beautiful grey eyes are so mesmerizing, I begin to fall into a trans. But no, shaking my head, I have to stay strong.

"My father is dead, and I have a sister and a brother?" he asks as if he doesn't believe the information.

"That's what it sounds like."

"I wonder if they know about me?"

"I don't know, but there's only one way to find out."

He looks up at me again, and there's a slight change in his stare. Somehow, I see hope and fear at the same time.

"Do you think I should reach out to them?" he asks hesitantly, fidgeting with his hands.

"I do, but it's not up to me. This has to be your decision. I can be there with you by your side, but the decision here is solely yours to make."

"I know; I just don't know what I should do. What if they resent me and want nothing to do with me?"

"That is a chance that you will have to take. I really think you should do it, though. If I had siblings out there, I would want to know them. They may have stories about your dad and want to come to the wedding. It would be nice to have some of your family members there."

"Yeah, you're right. Let's get some breakfast, and then I will make the call."

"Okay, babe. I will get Annabelle. It sounds like she's up anyways," hearing her cooing over the baby monitor.

We both get up. Bradley heads into the bathroom to freshen up, and I head to Annabelle's room.

"Hey, baby girl. How's my sweetheart doing this beautiful morning?"

She begins to blow spit bubbles and starts giggling. "Yeah, that's my baby girl. I love you too, precious." I pick her up and head into the kitchen. Bradley already made breakfast for the morning, so we sit at the island and eat together as a family.

"Okay, here goes nothing." Bradley grabs his phone and dials his sister's number. He puts it on speaker for me to hear as well.

"Hello?" someone answers.

"Hi, may I speak to Charlotte?"

"Speaking. May I ask who's calling?" Bradley takes a deep breath and begins to speak.

"My name is Bradley Philips—"

"Bradley, my brother, Bradley?" Charlotte interjects.

"Uh, yeah."

"Oh my gosh. I've waited for this day all my life," she gushes over the phone.

Bradley looks at me with absolute confusion and relief in his gaze, "Seriously?"

"Yeah, our father always talked about you but said we could never meet because he was very mean to your mother. I tried so many times to track you down, but I wasn't successful. I'm so glad you found me."

"Wow, I don't know what to say. I never knew I had a brother or a sister. It's a little weird that you know about me, but I don't know about y'all."

"Yeah, I can only imagine, but I've always wanted to meet you and be a part of your life. Please know that we've always prayed for this day, my brother and me. When our dad passed away, it made me want to know you even more."

"Uh, can I meet you somewhere?"

"Of course. Where do you live?"

"I now live in Savannah, Georgia, with my fiancé and daughter."

"Oh my gosh, you're getting married, and I'm an auntie? This is so exciting. I can come to you if that's, okay?" she exclaims.

"Sure, we have plenty of room. I will send you our address."

"Perfect. Wade is home for the weekend. He will be thrilled to come as well."

"Of course. I look forward to meeting you both."

They both hang up, and Bradley enters our address in a text for her. Tears start to run down his face, and I feel compelled to hold him in my arms.

I get up and snuggle my body between his legs wrapping my arms around his shoulders. He puts his head on my breast and starts crying harder.

"It's going to be okay, babe. This is a good thing. This is amazing news."

Sniffling, he wipes his tears on my shirt. "I know. I'm not upset; I just—this is a lot to take in. She knew who I was, and she'd been looking for me all this time, and I had no idea she even existed. This is crazy. He even admitted that he was shitty to my mother."

"I know it's fucked up, but something good is coming out of this. You have family out there, and they are more than willing to meet you. So, let's prepare for their arrival. Knowing all of our anticipations, they probably got on the road the second you hung up the phone."

"You're probably right. Let's get dressed." He picks me up and devours me with his lips, and I fall apart as I always do. He pulls away moments later, and I feel irrecoverable without his touch. "I can't wait to marry you."

"I can't wait to marry you either, Mr. Philips."

"Fuck this. I need you now." He carries me into the bedroom, leaving Annabelle in her play pin to entertain herself for a little while.

He presses me against the wall, lifts my dress, and thrusts his hard dick inside me. I scream at the intrusion, and he muffles my cries with his mouth.

Wrapping my legs around him, he thrust, and he thrust harder and harder. It's almost like he can't get enough of me and need more of me. So I give him all I have and let him take every ounce of my soul.

"Fuck Amelia. You feel fucking good, baby." He thrust again and again. I feel him swell inside me, and I know he's about to come.

Hell, I'm about to come as well with friction enticing my clit. This is the quickest we ever had sex before.

"Shit, baby, I'm about to come."

"Come, baby. I want to feel you come inside of me. Please," I beg.

And as always, he explodes inside me, we both sliding down the wall, onto the floor with my legs straddling him and me sitting in his lap. He's still coming inside me, filling me with his essences. I feel my pussy clenching his dick, and I never want to let go.

"I'm sorry, baby. I—I didn't mean to fuck you like that. I—just needed you bad," he pants between breaths.

"Babe, there's no need to apologize. My body belongs to you. You take what you need. I'm always here for you, no matter what."

"I know; I just want to treat you with respect."

"Who said you disrespected me? I wanted to fuck you as much as you wanted to fuck me. Hell, if I could tolerate it, I would fuck you all day, every day. Have you seen your dick? It's fucking massive."

We laugh, "So, you're using me for my dick?" Kissing me softly on my neck.

"And you're using me for my tight pussy."

"Touché."

"Now, go shower while I get Annabelle dressed and ready to meet her auntie and uncle."

"Right, Annabelle has an aunt and uncle. I have to get used to this."

"Well, she always had an auntie and uncle, but now she has more. So she will be spoiled rotten between our family and friends."

"You're right. This is so new to me. I didn't mean to belittle your family."

"I know what you meant. It's okay, babe. Stop worrying so much. I got you. That's what I'm here for, to remind you of things like this."

"Thanks, babe." He then smacks me on my ass, and I nearly jump out of my skin.

"Shit, that hurt, but it also felt good. I'm going to need you to do that more often."

We both smolder in our gazes. "No, we have to get dressed. We will never be ready if we keep jumping each other's bones."

"Okay, okay. I will take a shower, and then I will watch Annabelle so you can take a shower and get ready.""

"Thanks, babe."

"No, thank you."

CHAPTER 29

BRADLEY

I'm like a kid in a candy store, so giddy and anxious. Of course, I'm a fucking nervous wreck, and I don't need to be. I need to grow some balls and stop being a little bitch about meeting my sister and brother.

Taking a deep breath and letting it out, the doorbell rings.

Fuck they're here.

"They're here, babe. I'm so excited," Amelia announces from the foyer.

"I'm glad one of us is. I'm losing my shit over here."

She laughs, but this shit isn't funny. "Babe, calm down. You will be fine," she reassures me. She opens the door, greets my sister and brother, and invites them to come in. She's so good at this. I take a deep breath and walk over to the door to greet them.

In walks a beautiful young woman. She has long, wavy hair flowing down her back and beautiful brown skin. Her eyes are the very eyes I look at every morning of every day, stormy grey skies on an eerily wintery day. She is shorter than me but much taller than Amelia. She looks like she's very athletic yet stylish and slightly conservative.

I extend my hand out to greet her, "Hi, Charlotte, I'm —" she pulls me into an embrace and hugs me tightly and firmly, catching me off guard.

"I'm more of a hugger; I don't shake hands," Charlotte says.

"Uh, okay," I hesitantly hug her back. This shit feels a little bizarre.

Followed behind her is a young man about the same height as me. He has an excellent brush cut with a full beard, making him look older. He has those same eyes Charlotte, and I share, and I immediately connect with him more than I do Charlotte. He stands like me, confident and strong. He presents himself like me, well-mannered and mature. I see much of myself in him.

"Hey Wade, how's it going?"

"Good bro, good." He holds his hand out, and I take it proudly, pulling him into a brotherly embrace. I then release him and invite them to come into the living area where Annabelle plays in her play pin.

"Oh my gosh, is this my niece?" Charlotte exclaims. Looking over her shoulder at me.

"Yes, this is Annabelle. She just turned one earlier this month," I say.

"She's so precious. Her long curls and beautiful eyes."

"Yeah, bro. You're gonna have to keep a gun handy. She will break plenty of hearts," Wade expresses.

"Don't I know it," I agree.

We all sit down, and Amelia brings us lemonade.

"Thank you," Charlotte says as she takes a glass. "Y'all have a beautiful home. I've always loved visiting Savannah. Such a beautiful place."

"Yes, it is. I was born and raised here. I love it here," Amelia proclaims.

"This is so weird," I say aloud before I know it.

"Yeah, this is a little overwhelming. I assumed you knew about us too when you called, but I realized quickly that is not the case after speaking with you," Charlotte agrees.

"Yeah. My mom died a few months ago, so when I found out the truth about my father, I wanted to confront him, so I hired someone to help me find him, but instead of finding him alive, I found more than I bargained for. At first, I was upset that I couldn't speak to my father, but then I became more hurt for not knowing I had a sister and a brother all this time, and y'all lived so close to me, and I had no idea. So I'm a little blowed, but also fortunate to have a family. If that makes any sense."

"Dude, we felt the same way for years. We knew we had a brother but could never meet him. It was both frustrating and utter bullshit. And of course, when we challenged our dad about it, he finally told us the truth of what happened to you and your mother. It was fucking awful, and for a long time, I resented our dad for it. Honestly, I think the stress from all the shit he did is what really killed him, but whatever," Wade spits out.

"Wade, you shouldn't talk about him like that. He really tried," Charlotte urges.

"Yeah, whatever. He was a dick; you just didn't see it because you didn't want to see it," Wade points out.

"So, what did he really do? I really don't know. My mother said he left a long time ago and never returned. She never told me the reason."

"Fuck, are you sure you want to know?" Wade asks, running his hand across his waves.

"Yes, I'm sure."

"Okay, here goes nothing."

"Wade!" Charlotte cuts him off.

"Stop Charlotte, it's time," Wade waving her off. "When I was about fourteen, I found pictures of a woman tied to a bed, naked with bruises all over her. It was so disturbing; I showed Charlotte first before we went to our mom and dad. Apparently, he would beat and starve your mother, tie her to the bed and make her watch him fuck other women. He then had those other women take pictures of her to admire his handy work. Our fucked-up mother was a part of the whole thing at one point until she supposedly changed her life around when she got pregnant with Charlotte. I hated the fucker since then, and I haven't spoken to my mother either. They are fucking freaks, and I never want to be a part of that life, ever."

"Wade," Charlotte chastises with her tone.

"No, fuck that. He needs to hear the truth. And you need to fucking stop defending those assholes," Wade spits back.

"All this time, I had no idea. My mother kept all of this from me. Probably because she was afraid and/or ashamed. I think she knew I probably would have killed him if I found out. I can't believe this shit," shaking my head in disbelief. Amelia squeezes my hand to comfort me. There's nothing more she can really do other than give me strength through this shit right here.

"Bradley, please understand. Our father did some horrible things, but I believe he and my mother have changed over the years. They started going to church and gave their lives to God. I was distraught when Wade and I discovered what happened, but I've watched them. They were no longer like that. They're no longer the same people who took those photos."

I look at her, stunned at her response to this whole fucked up situation. "Bradley, before you respond. Please let me put Annabelle in her crib first, and I would like to say something," Amelia looks into my eyes, pleading with me to not say what I'm obviously thinking. I want to ignore her so badly, but I listen to her and sit here trying my damnedest to calm the fuck down. Finally, she picks Annabelle up and takes her into the nursery. I sit there staring at everything else, but my apparent sister, the person I want to fucking choke to death.

Moments later, Amelia walks in and sits next to me again.

"Okay, I know, Bradley. He's about to lose his mind, and before that happens, I would like to say something." She looks at the three of us, and we give her permission to speak, which she really doesn't need but asks anyway. "Look, I think I can speak on this subject because my sister and my best friend experienced the same thing Bradley's mother apparently experienced." Shit, I forgot all about that.

"No one can ever imagine what it's like to be held against your will, raped, beaten, humiliated in front of God knows who, and then left for dead in front of your impressionable young son. No one. So, for you to sit here and tell Bradley that your mother and your father had a fucking change of heart is not only disrespectful but also hurtful in so many ways. Now, I get it. You're looking for any type of good that your mother and father might have had, but in reality, they did what they did. So, please don't try to convince us that everything is okay now. Bradley is experiencing this all for the first time. You two have had years to get over this, and it's undeniable that you more so than Wade has forgiven them, but please do not force him to feel something that he has not had the time nor the energy to feel." Holy shit! My fiancé is a badass. Now, that's what I'm talking about. I need a woman who will have my back and save me from going to fucking jail. Ryan and Jason were right.

Charlotte drops her head in her hands, "I'm so sorry. I didn't mean to try to sway your feelings or hurt you more than you already feel. I just—"

"You were hoping that I would forgive your mother and father and not judge you for what they did," I speak up.

"Yeah," she looks up with hope in her eyes again.

"I don't judge you, nor do I feel that you are responsible for what your parents did to my mother; however, I shall never forgive that asshole or your mother, for that matter, for torturing my mother. That's something that cannot and will not be forgiven."

"See, Charlotte. It's not just me. He feels the same way and to think, I had time to get over it, and I'm still not over it," Wade adds.

"Look, let's not gang up on Charlotte. I understand wanting to see the good in people. I'm the same way, but life has taught me that some evil people don't deserve our love or our forgiveness. Trust me, I know," Amelia admits. "However, Charlotte, you must see where we are coming from, right?"

Charlotte nods her head in defeat but also contemplates Amelia's statement.

"She's right. Her family has been through a lot over the years, and still, she stands strong and committed to helping others and taking care of her family, our family," I correct myself. "And I would like both of you to be a part of our family. We're getting married this weekend and hope you can come if possible. I would love to have someone represent me on my side," I chuckle.

"Of course, bro. Count me in," Wade agrees.

"Yes, I will be there as well. We just need to find a hotel," Charlotte suggests.

"Nonsense. We have plenty of room here. We have two extra rooms, well one is a dance studio, but we can easily convert it into a bedroom. Did y'all bring an overnight bag?"

"No, we were too excited to come to see our big bro," Wade admits. "But I'm sure we can go pick up a thing or two."

"Absolutely. I'll take you both down Broughton Street. The good thing about this area is we live right above the shops and clubs."

"Hell yeah. Sounds like I'm going out tonight," Wade exclaims, rubbing his palms together. "You coming, bro?"

"Uh—"

"Yes, he'll go. Charlotte and I can stay home and watch Annabelle. Go spend time with your brother." I look at Amelia with adoration. Sometimes I wonder how I got so damn lucky.

"Yeah, I want to play with my niece and get to know my future sister-in-law," Charlotte agrees. She's lucky Amelia was here because I was about to fucking bury her in her own backyard. But I'm going to leave it alone and walk the fuck away from this before I do something stupid.

"Wade, let's head out and let the ladies catch up. My homeboy took me to a men's store down the street. You may like what they have."

"Here, Wade, use my credit card. Get—" Charlotte offers, but I cut her off.

"No need. I will take care of the expenses," I say with authority in my voice. Probably more than I should have.

"Oh, okay. Wade, don't go overboard," putting her credit card back in her purse.

"Yes, mother," Wade says sarcastically, rolling his eyes.

We then head out before she can say anything else.

We take the elevator to the ground floor. There's no need to take the car because the store is literally a couple of blocks away. And besides, this will give me a chance to pick my little bro's head, get to know him a little better.

"Sorry about that. Sis can be a little overbearing, but she means well. Ever since our parents started heading south with their health, she feels the need to be over-protective of me for some reason."

"How is your mother doing?"

"Worse. She's been an alcoholic for years, so now her mind is going, and she has no idea who we are, let alone who she is. It's actually fucking pathetic. But like I tell my or our sister, she deserves everything she gets," he says with obvious disdain for his mother.

231

"Wow, you feel very strongly about what your parents did to my mom."

"It's disgusting. How do you teach us what's right and wrong when you clearly had no idea from the jump. They're fucking hypocrites, and I'm sick and tired of it. I strive to be the very opposite of my parents. Now, I'm a senior in college and interning at a major financial company based in Atlanta."

"It's crazy that you're in finance because that's what I'm getting my degree in. Well, I finished online, but nonetheless, we're studying the same thing. I work for a major finance company here in Savannah and hope to be partners soon."

"Shit, that's great, bro. See, I knew we would connect. I had a feeling. When I was younger, I would pray you would come over and play with me when my…uh our sister would get on my last nerve."

We both laugh, "I can only imagine."

"Oh, she's great, she just overthinks everything, and it can be fucking annoying sometimes."

We enter the clothing store, and his eyes light up. He has a cool mentality about himself, laid back, but also playful in a way.

"They got some cool stuff in here, but on the expensive side. Are you sure you want to shop here? My sister…uh our sister would kill me if she found out you spent too much money on me."

"What she doesn't know won't kill her. Besides, she can't tell me how to spend my money."

"Cool. You said nothing but a thang. Let's get started," with a bit of pep in his step.

He grabs a few things, plus some boxers and tees and a pair of shoes. Overall, he spent less than I ever could imagine for a guy his age. But, whatever. I'm good with whatever. They don't know that I'm a millionaire, and I'm not ready to tell them just yet. I would like to get to know them first.

"We also need to get a suit for the wedding. It's on Saturday."

"Okay, bet. What do you think I should get?"

"We're wearing khaki linen because it's so hot in Savannah, even if we're in the middle of October."

"Yeah, at least we have a breeze in Jacksonville. Here, it's just muggy as hell."

"Who you tellin', but my wife loves it here, so I gotta get used to it."

"Your wife, huh?"

"Well, she will be my wife in a couple of days; why not claim it now."

"I feel ya. She's a pretty cool chick. Hell, she stood up to Charlotte, a slam dunk in my book."

"I see. She seems a little affirmative."

"Just a little? Please, she has always tried her best to run my life. From trying to make me go to school closer to home to who I should date. It's actually fucking ridiculous, and that's why I left and went to Atlanta for school. I needed to find my own way without the stigmatism of being just like my daddy," throwing up air quotes.

"Honestly, I never even inquired about the guy until my mother passed away and I met with her lawyer. He said some pretty alarming shit to me, so I figured I would find him and get his side of the story. Other than that, he was dead to me. It never crossed my mind that he would father other children. Hell, he couldn't take care of the first one he had; why make life harder by having not one but two more kids."

"Yeah, I wondered the same. He wasn't exactly the fatherly type. Why have kids if you don't want them?" Wade places his items on the counter for the clerk to ring them up.

The clerk rings up the items and I hand him my credit card.

"Thank you, sir, and you will be seeing me again," I say to the clerk behind the counter.

"Absolutely, Mr. Philips," the clerk welcomes.

"Wow, they know you by name?"

"I was just in here a couple of days ago. So he might just remember me from then."

"Oh, okay. Anyways, what you get into around here?"

"There's a nice lounge bar about a block or two up the street. The guys took me there a couple of times. It's actually pretty nice."

"Bet. That's where we're headed tonight."

"Cool. Let's head back. I like to be home for dinner with Amelia."

"You really love her, don't you?"

"Yeah, I do. The moment I laid eyes on her a year ago, I knew I had to have her."

"That's cool, man. I'm nowhere ready to settle down, but I want what you have when I am."

"Give it time. You will find it. My first girlfriend was my first love, but things started going downhill when Annabelle came along. I had to protect my daughter."

"Hell, I don't blame you with all you been through. First, you lost your mother, and now you find out you lost your father. Protect your daughter by all means. I'm just shocked that I have a niece. Now I have a reason to kick somebody's ass if they come sideways."

We both laugh and head back to the house. While walking, Lamonte pulls up next to us in his marked unit.

"Hey man, what's up?"

"Nothing really, taking my little bro out tonight? When's your shift over?"

"Seven. What y'all getting into?"

"We gonna check out the JW. See what's poppin' off."

"Bet, I'll get at y'all later. Call Jason and Ryan. See if they're busy. You need a bachelor's party anyway."

"Man, not tonight—"

"Pull your panties out yo ass. It's going down tonight."

He then drives off before I can protest.

"Fuck, I'm not in the mood for the pussy-poppin' lap dances. I got all I need at home."

"Yes, but this is more for letting your hair down sort of speak. Besides, I won't let you get caught up. Just hand the chick over to me. I'll take her off your hands," rubbing his hands together like he about to get into some shit.

"Fine, but I don't need these problems right now."

"I got you, bro."

CHAPTER 30

AMELIA

"So, do you have any kids or a boyfriend or a husband?" I ask Charlotte while we sit on the balcony drinking wine and watching Annabelle play with her toys.

"Uh, no to all. I've always wanted kids; I just haven't found the right person yet. Men can be dicks sometimes, and I don't have time to play games."

"Well, not all men are dicks. I'm just glad I found a good one. People say it's rare to find your true love the first go around."

"Yeah, you're lucky. I've been through several duds. So, what's my brother like?" she asks with enthusiasm and anticipation.

"Well, he's very charming and respectable. He's a loving father, and he always puts our needs before his own. He's brilliant, definitely good with numbers. He loved his mother dearly and did not want to leave her, but she insisted on him living his life and creating a better life for his daughter."

"Yeah, whatever happened to Annabelle's mother?"

"Uh, well—"

"Hey babe, you missed me?" Bradley enters the balcony just in time, cutting me off. I really didn't want to answer her questions since I was responsible for killing Annabelle's mother, which has haunted me since.

"Of course, I missed you, but weren't you supposed to spend time with Wade?"

"Trying to get rid of me, I see," he kisses me on the cheek and starts tickling me, knowing I hate being tickled.

"No, stop, babe!" I protest.

"I'll stop if you kiss me."

"Okay, okay." I kiss him on the lips, and I can feel myself melting in his arms.

"Get a room," Wade teases. We all start cackling.

"What are y'all up to?" Wade asks.

"Nothing, just getting to know each other. She will be my sister-in-law after all, so I would like to know who's joining the family," Charlotte states proudly.

"Yeah, right. You just trying to be nosy. Anyways, we need to get dressed. We're headed to some rooftop at the JW with Bradley's boys," Wade says.

"Oh, yes. I love that Rooftop. They play a variety of music and have a great lounge area. It's been a while since I've been there, but I know it's still the same, great drinks and plenty of people to meet."

"Oh, really?" Bradley challenges.

"Yes. I was single once. I know what Wade wants."

"That's right. I like you already. Thanks, sis. Good lookin' out," Wade agrees.

"Any time. We're family now."

"Don't have too much —" Charlotte says, but Wade cuts her off.

"Back off, sis. I'm a grown man. Let me be."

"He'll be with me. I'll make sure he's okay. Besides, he's in good hands. I used to be a cop," Bradley announces proudly.

"Holy shit, you were them folks?" Wade questions.

"I prefer cop. But okay, yes, for four years. I got out after a huge case I was working."

"Bro. That's cool as shit. We need to talk."

"We got plenty of time to talk, but first, let's get the hell outta here before the boys think I'm being a pussy."

The guys head back in the house, and once again, the interrogation starts from Charlotte.

"So, you never answered the question?"

"That's a question for your brother, and I'll leave it at that."

"Okay, I understand. I'll talk with him."

Feeling a little uncomfortable, I come up with an excuse to leave. I know she wants information about her brother, but I'm not the one she needs to be asking. Instead, she needs to sit down with Bradley.

"Hey, it's getting late and past Annabelle's bedtime. My home is your home. If you need anything, just let me know. I've placed towels and wash cloths on the bed."

"Sure, but isn't this my brother's house?" I look her in her eyes with an apparent glare in my gaze and disdain in my stance. "I mean, I just thought this was his house."

"No, it's my house; however, what's mine is his and vice versa. Now, if you would excuse me."

"I didn't mean any harm. I just don't understand why he's not marrying Tyra."

I turn around and glower at her because I know damn well I did not mention Tyra's name. "How do you know her name?"

"I must have heard you or Bradley saying it."

"No, you didn't, so I will ask again before I kindly put your ass out of my house."

"Okay, okay. Bradley doesn't know, but Tyra was a good friend of mine. We went to school together, and we always had a crush on Bradley. I had no idea he was my brother until after we graduated, but it was too late then. I lost contact with Tyra and never seen Bradley again."

I sit back down because this confession just blew me away. "So, you're saying you had a crush on your brother, but your friend got to him first?"

"Uh, to put it kindly, yeah. It sounds a little disturbing," we both burst out laughing.

"Uh, yeah. Just a tad bit. Can you imagine dating your brother, having sex with your brother, and then having a child with your brother. Ha, that shit would have been crazy. You need to tell him."

"Oh, no. I'm not telling him I had a crush on him in school. Are you freaking crazy?"

"Probably, but he would want to know. Trust me. He hates secrets, and he has had his share of them lately."

"I guess you're right, but how do I tell my brother I had a crush on him in high school?"

Just then, Bradley and Wade walk back into the house, probably because they forgot something.

"You what?" Wade snarl. She looks up at them, and you can see the panic flash across her face, blood pooling in the pit of her stomach.

"I, uh, I—"

"You what?" Bradley scowls also.

A pause that seemed to last forever sliced through the room. I stand up and walk over to Bradley.

239

"Babe, I think you and your sister need to talk."

"I can see that. But, Charlotte, what do you mean you had a crush on your brother?"

"Uh, I, uh. Shit, I can't do this. I—I." She places her head in her hands, and for the first time, I see fear in her demeanor. First, she seemed so put together, but now I can see that was just a front.

"Here, Bradley. Sit. Wade, sweetie, you too." They both sit down and wait for an explanation. "Charlotte knew you in high school but did not know you were her brother until after you graduated. You see, she was best friend with Tyra, and they both had crushes on you. But it seems that you were more interested in Tyra than Charlotte. Unfortunately, it was too late by the time she figured out you were her brother. You and Tyra graduated already, and she lost contact with Tyra." Bradley stares me in the eyes with confusion in his expression. I see the wheels turning, and when the very second he realizes the story is true, he turns to his sister.

"Holy fuck! Charlotte. Thee Charlotte! I can't believe this. You were that close to me, and I had no idea. Tyra talked about you often but said you two were not friends anymore because of a misunderstanding. She was so hurt that there were times I caught her crying. She never told me what happened with the two of you, but I knew it was serious."

"She was my best friend, and you were the hot, sexy baseball player. And, not to mention you were a year older than me. I was the nerdy junior, and you both were seniors," Charlotte glances at her feet.

"Sis, why didn't you tell me any of this? You knew I wanted to find our brother. He was right there, and you said nothing," Wade questions.

"I didn't know he was our brother at the time. I had my yearbook sitting out on my bed one day when dad saw it. He glanced at the book, and suddenly, his skin turned pale grey, and his demeanor changed from thoughtfulness to fear. He looked like he saw a ghost. I asked him what was wrong, but he just ignored me and walked out. I then grabbed the yearbook and looked at what he was looking at, and sure enough, he was staring at Bradley, my secret crush, and his son. I never seen it before, but Bradley had our eyes, and he looked just like you, Wade," tears running down her face, her hands trembling, reaching out for him. "Wade, I didn't know what to do. I tried calling Tyra, but she was so mad at me that she refused to answer any of my calls, so I decided to let it go. I'm so sorry. I was stupid and young. I didn't mean to hurt anyone, especially you, Wade."

Wade backing from her, torn between present and past. "I can't believe this! I can't believe you! You knew all this time and said nothing," Wade yells.

"I was trying to protect you and our family. Besides, I was young and stupid. I cared more about losing my crush than finding out that he was my brother. I know it was a selfish thing to do, but that's the truth."

"Well, you know what, sis, fuck you! Fuck dad, and fuck mom! Y'all deserve everything you get. Bradley is a fucking human being, and y'all treated him and his mother like they were beneath you. I can't believe I was born into a fucked-up family," Wade spits out and turns to Bradley. "I need to get out of here. Brad, man, bro, I'm sorry you're going through this. But I can't be here anymore."

"Yeah, fucking leave like you always do. You're just as much a coward as I am," Charlotte snaps back through sobs.

"Fuck you, Charlotte. I'm not a coward; I just refuse to be around fucked-up people such as yourself."

"Please don't leave Wade. We want you here, right, Bradley?" I plead with him, looking to Bradley for guidance. Bradley glances at me and realizes what I'm asking, urging him to stop Wade from leaving.

"Uh, yes, of course," shaking his head. "You don't have to leave, and I'm not mad at either one of you. Has this been a shity revelation on all our parts? Yes, but it doesn't have to define who we are. Our parents made decisions for us that changed our lives up until now, but we don't have to let it destroy us. You're still my sister," he looks at Charlotte. "And you're my brother. I never want to lose contact with either of you. I think we can fix what our parents broke."

I look at Bradley, and, in this moment, I understand why I'm genuinely in love with him and why I want to marry him. He's a remarkable, loving person, and he would do anything in his power to make things right with his siblings. Hell, he would do anything for Annabelle and me, so I shouldn't think any less of him. This has been a year from hell, but it has also taught us many things and has definitely brought Bradley and me closer together. The guys decided to stay home, even though Bradley boys had plans for him tonight. But I feel it's crucially important for Bradley to remain with his family, and he agreed. So, therefore, we all had a glass of wine on the balcony enjoying each other's company, not really saying another word to each other.

EPILOGUE

BRADLEY

The day has come when I will marry the love of my life. This feeling I have cannot be described. It's nothing like the feeling I had with Tyra. With her, it was more of an obligation to love her because she carried my child. Not because I genuinely loved her like I'm in love with Amelia. We have a passion I never experienced before and a connection that can never be broken. Hell, Annabelle loved her the moment she set eyes on Amelia; it just took me a little longer to figure it out.

We're at Amelia's childhood home, and I find myself wanting to give her the same type of home that shaped her and molded her into the person she is today. We both have been through a hell of a ride, but now we can say we can survive anything if we're together.

I'm pacing back and forth in the backyard when I realize I haven't read the letter my mother left me. Why this letter is setting so heavy on my soul now, is beyond me, but I think it's fine time I read it. Find out what my mother couldn't say all those years ago.

I pull the enveloped letter out of my coat pocket. Placing it there every day gives me a reminder of how precious life is. I glance at it with hope and fear in my soul. I have to find out what she wanted to tell me. It's time.

I open it up and read the first line.

My dearest boy…

I immediately shut my eyes, trying to give myself strength to read more. Taking a deep breath…

My dearest boy,

On that chilling morning of December 23, you came into this world and sweetened up my life. I can't thank God enough for the treasure bestowed upon me. My dearest son, you will always be my number one.

You've grown up to be a fine young man, and I can't be more proud. Remember all the things that I've taught you. Always know that I will always love you till my last breath.

Cherish our family values of love, respect, hard work, and sacrifice and always put your family first. Raising a family is not a walk in the park, my dearest son. You'll be faced with challenges along the way, but I know you'll always rise to the challenge.

I know you have questions about your father and know I never meant to hurt you by keeping him from you. I knew he would eventually kill me, taking you from me forever, and I couldn't live with that, ever.

So, I ran.

He did horrific things to me and I never wanted you to see or learn of the cruelty your father put me through. No one should have to go through those horrible things, not even you. Therefore, I made the decision to run, to hide, to cover my identity from everyone. To hide the truth from everyone to protect you, my dearest son.

If you're reading this, I've left this earth and joined the other side. With that being said, take the money I've saved for you and your children. Know that I will always be there for you no matter what. You can lean on me whenever you feel down. Take comfort in the fact that you'll overcome all obstacles that life puts in your way.

Find a young, beautiful, smart woman who will cherish you and your children. Tyra ain't it if you haven't figured that out by now. Grow with her, love her, and help her. You deserve to be happy.

If have the strength, forgive your father. I have. Drugs, money, and power makes people do crazy things and that's why I wanted a simple life for you and me. Don't be mad that I didn't tell you about our wealth. Your grandparents were extraordinary financial analyst. Probably why you're so good with numbers. I didn't want your father to destroy or piss away all they worked hard for. But I know now, I should've never kept that away from you. I was just young, scared, and a little naive at the time.

Please forgive me and know without a doubt, you were truly loved. Please take care of my little Annabelle.

Love you always

Mom

My god, my mother knew everything and experienced everything and still she put me first. Tears streaming down my face and me pacing back and forth, my brother, Wade, and my sister, Charlotte, approach me.

"Hey bro, you look like you're running a marathon in this backyard. Calm down; she isn't going anywhere," Wade tries to soothe me. I stuff the letter back into my coat pocket and try to gather my wits.

"Yeah, Amelia is a lovely young lady; she will kill before she has to give you up." I look up at Charlotte and stare her in the eyes at her choice of words. We never discussed Tyra and what happened to her, but I think she figured it out, just by the comments she be making.

"Yeah, she probably would," I agree. "She's upstairs getting ready if you want to hang out with the girls."

"I think I will have a chat with my sister-in-law. After all, she saved my brother and protected my niece with her life. She is family," Charlotte confesses.

She turns off before I can say another word. She has some damn good investigative skills, but I knew that already, being a prosecutor and all.

"You never know what to expect from Charlotte, but she's very loyal and dedicated to family. Give her a chance; she will turn out to be a good sister even when she's too much to handle," Wade offers.

"I'm starting to see that."

"You ready?"

"Been ready my whole life. With Tyra, it never crossed my mind to settle down completely. I was at the peak of my career and that's all I really thought about. I didn't want to marry her and I'm just glad I never did. With Amelia, I can't breathe without her. I can't think without her, and with her, I'm whole. She has always been there for Annabelle and me, and there isn't enough shit in the world that would make up for everything she has done for me, but this right here, this is meant to be. This is everything." I know I sound like a pussy boy, but when it comes to Amelia, nothing will ever stop me from loving her, nothing.

"Wow, man. I hope I find someone like that."

"Oh, you will, and when you do, never let her go."

"Shit, no. I will kill a motha-fucker before I let that happen."

We both chuckle and head out to the backyard.

"Holy shit, Kim, Dianella, and Lily have really outdone themselves. This is incredible. Amelia is going to be so happy when she sees this."

"Yeah, she will, but first, we have to take our places. Those group of women look mean as hell. I don't want to piss them off."

"Right, let's do this."

I stand at the altar with Reverend Carter. Amelia says the pastor is very close to the family, and she wouldn't have anyone else to marry us off. I'm ready to be married to the most beautiful, loving woman in the world; I don't really care who pronounce us husband and wife, as long as it happens.

As we wait for my bride to arrive, I listen to soft music in the corner of the yard. It's not traditional tunes you hear at all weddings. No, this is a more authentic type of music. As a matter of fact, it's the same music Amelia was dancing to when she was in her studio. My mind starts drifting to that night, and I remember how mesmerized I was when she lured me into her world. Annabelle was enticed by her dancing as well. My mind then drifts to the first moment I set eyes on the most beautiful, purest heart in the world. I knew I had to have her in my life at that very moment.

The music stops, and I look up. I'm not nervous; I'm not scared. This moment is what I prayed about every waking second of the day. Then the most amazing thing happens, and I watch my world change forever at this moment.

In a gown of the purest white feathers, I've ever seen flows around the most angelic soul in the world. At this moment, she looks so heavenly that I almost feel like this is a dream. She drifts down the aisle of beautiful greenery and white flowers spread all over the backyard. Her dress has these very thin straps, showing her beautiful copper skin. Her hair is pinned up with curls surrounding her face and flowing down her back. She's carrying beautiful white lilies in her hands as she continues to glide closer to the alter. Her eyes are full of life, and for a moment, I forget that there are several other people here to witness our fellowship. I hear Annabelle to the side of me, which takes me out of my trans. The love of my life will soon forever be my wife.

ALSO BY NICOLETTE JOHNSON

Don't forget to indulge in the first two novels in the *Handcuffed* Series:

Handcuffed

Shackled

Let me know how you like the series thus far

Facebook @authornicolettejohnson

Twitter @PenNicoletteJo

Instagram @authornicolette

www.authornicolettejohnson.com

Read in order:

Handcuffed

Shackled

Bounded

(Coming Soon)

Entangled

www.ingramcontent.com/pod-product-compliance
Lightning Source LLC
Chambersburg PA
CBHW070750280626
47162CB00018B/2823